The Thr

WITHDRAWN

Also by Jo Ann Yolanda Hernández

White Bread Competition

The Throwaway Piece

Jo Ann Yolanda Hernández

Arte Público Press
Houston, Texas

The Throwaway Piece is made possible in part from grants from the City of Houston through The Cultural Arts Council of Houston/Harris County, the University of California at Irvine Chicano/Latino Literary Prize and by the Exemplar Program, a program of Americans for the Arts in Collaboration with the LarsonAllen Public Services Group, funded by the Ford Foundation.

Piñata Books are full of surprises!

Piñata Books

An imprint of
Arte Público Press
University of Houston
452 Cullen Performance Hall
Houston, Texas 77204-2004

Cover design and illustration by Giovanni Mora

Hernández, Jo Ann Yolanda
    The Throwaway Piece / Jo Ann Yolanda Hernández.
        p. cm.
    Summary: Even after entering the foster care system, Jewel is the one who takes care of her mother and, shutting herself off from the vulnerability of closeness to others, is unaware of the positive influence she has on those around her.
    ISBN-10: 1-55885-353-7(alk. paper)
    ISBN-13: 978-1-55885-353-9
    [1. Self-esteem—Fiction. 2. Foster home care—Fiction. 3. Abused women—Fiction. 4. Mothers and daughters—Fiction.] I. Title.
PZ7.H43177Thr 2006
[Fic]—dc22   2005044749
                                                                      CIP

♾ The paper used in this publication meets the requirements of the American National Standard for Information Sciences—Permanence of Paper for Printed Library Materials, ANSI Z39.48-1984.

6 7 8 9 0 1 2 3 4 5   10 9 8 7 6 5 4 3 2 1

Rule #1
What's important is never you

I didn't start out as a State Kid. Name's Jewel. When I was four, my mom and I lived in an apartment complex with an inner courtyard, where the smells of everyone's supper mingled: boiled cabbage, roasted *jalapeños*, and spaghetti sauce.

My mom and I squeezed into three rooms and a kitchenette with smoke-stained paint, smudged fingerprints around the door-knobs, and bars on the windows. Neighbors became privy to each other's lives through apartment walls. People turned up their televisions to drown out kids who screamed for mercy or maybe love. Families made do with what they had and dreamed their hope-driven dreams of what could be.

"Mommy, where you going?"

"Out."

"Why?"

"Because."

"'Cause why?"

"Because you're such a little question box."

I stand next to the dresser, my hands locked on the edge, barely able to see over the top. In my jean overalls and a yellow shirt, I watch my mother in the mirror lining her green eyes with makeup. "So you be pretty."

"Jewel, I've told you to stop speaking like that. We want our new daddy to be proud of us. You have to speak proper English." Mom smiles into the mirror and blows me a kiss.

1

I catch the kiss and pat my cheek, enjoying the game she plays with me. If I can keep Mom playing, maybe she won't leave me alone.

"You're the most beautiful daughter a mother could have." Mom's waist-length black hair shimmers as she bends forward to color her lips. She smacks at her pale reflection and sucks in her cheeks.

I don't smile. The worry feeling leeches into my body as the stomps of the Dragon get loud. I saw him in a book, and now he haunts the nights when Mommy is gone.

When my mom is stronger, I'll be able to tell her about the Dragon. She'll chase it away. For now, I have to be brave.

"I wanna go."

Mom tilts her head and winks at me. "No. This is grown-up playtime. Maybe tomorrow we can do something. Would you like to go to the park?"

I nod, then crawl on top of Mom's double bed. The one place the Dragon can't come. Mom crosses the room and picks a dress from the closet.

"What about this one, honey bunch?" She holds the outfit up by the hanger. A scarlet-sequined dress, short-sleeved, split up the side, sparkles in the light.

I smile. I like the color red. "You gonna bring me home a daddy?" This is Mom's favorite game.

Mom pulls the dress over her head, still talking. She pops her head out of the top. "Tonight's the night, kid. The love potion is going to work. I've this strong feeling tonight is going to be magic."

I kneel and bounce on the bed, clapping my hands. "I like magic shows."

Mom struggles with the clasps on the back of her dress. "Yeah, your kind of magic's fun, but it doesn't pay the bills."

I hate the word "bills." It makes the sound of my mother's voice sad and sometimes mean. What would we be like with a daddy? Would he pay the bills? I flop forward and lie on my stomach, my feet in the air. I spy the face of the Dragon in the mirror, but the image is gone before my mother looks up.

She checks her watch, which has her name, Angela, spelled in diamond chips across the band. From the closet, she pulls out silver strap heels, sits down next to me, and strokes my cheek.

"One day we're going to meet a magic prince. He's going to take us away, out of this tenement, to live in a fabulous house."

I ask more to keep the dream going and my mother from leaving. "Will I have toys? And dolls?" I roll over, hang my head off the bed and, upside down, watch my mother strap the heels to her ankles.

"Yes, you'll have your own room, filled with toys, dolls, everything your heart desires. I'll have a room to do my artwork. I won't have to work at the drugstore because he will be very successful. People will respect him. Every time they meet me, they'll treat me well because I'm his wife. Other fine ladies will invite me to their homes to play bridge."

"What's bridge, Mommy?" I knot my forehead.

"It's a game your new daddy will teach me. He'll like to teach me a lot of things so he can be really proud of me. I'll learn fast." My mother stands to check herself in the mirror and runs her hands over her flat stomach and her trim hips.

I feel the Dragon's hot breath on my legs. "Are you leaving me?" I search for magic words to keep my mother near.

"It's time, sweetheart." My mother swings me onto her hip. She steps out into the hallway and walks on a once blue, now gray, strip of carpet. It runs the length of the hallway with worn-out spots in front of each doorway.

The hallway lightbulb has been out since last week and, like my mother says, the paycheck isn't due for several more days.

Light from my mother's bedroom fades into the gray by the time we reach my room. My ears fill with the snorts from the Dragon. I bury my face in my mother's neck.

She gives me an extra tight squeeze when she feels me tremble. "Silly girl. Mommy won't let the boogeyman get you. I promise. I'll never let anything hurt you."

My mother squeezes me too tight, and I feel my breath caught in my body. This hug is more for her than for me, so I wrap my chubby arms around my mother's neck. "I love you, Mommy."

She flips on the light of my bedroom. A small white bed comes into view. She sets me on the bed, helps me undress, and slips my pajamas over my head. "When you get older, you'll be able to help me more by doing this yourself."

I grab and pull my pajama top down hard to get rid of the wrinkles. I check to see if my mother notices.

She reaches over the bed, and I fill my nose with her perfume. She snatches a three-foot-long purple feather from the nightstand. I stand on the bed, and she waves the plume over me. "Evil spirits away with you. Only angels and good fairies visit my daughter tonight," she chants.

I jump from the bed and open the closet door. My mother shakes the feather at every corner. I shut the door and rush to lift the skirt of my bed. With the purple feather, my mother sweeps the floor beneath the bed and chants. I giggle as I stand at the door to the hallway. She wiggles the feather around the doorway, then tickles me all over my body.

I run around her, and she chases me onto the bed. I bounce on my bed, and she replaces the feather in the jar next to the lamp.

My mother fluffs the pillow and slips the covers over my doll and me. I grip the ribboned edges of the blanket.

"Dream good dreams tonight, baby." She kisses me on the cheek.

I touch my cheek and feel the sticky lipstick. "I don't wanna be alone."

She stops at the door; her shoulders stiffen into corners. "If you need anything, you just go next door. Mrs. Flores will let you in, but she'll charge me if you go over."

I stretch my arms out to my mommy. "I'm sad when you're gone."

She stands at the doorway, sparkling in the light. "I know, honey. I'm sorry." She turns around. "Mommy has to go. You want Mommy to find a new daddy, don't you?" The whine in her voice is as loud as mine.

I wipe my nose with the back of my hand.

My mom sighs, goes to the bathroom, and comes back clutching toilet paper. "Wipe your nose. I count on my big girl to help me out. I can count on you, can't I? You understand why I have to go. I'm doing this for you as much as myself."

I bury my face in the tissue and blow. She takes the knotted wad from me and drops it into the basket next to my bed.

"I'm so very proud of you." My mom tucks the sheet around my shoulders. "The best daughter in the whole wide world. I love you, sweetie." She kisses my forehead. "You have to be the best daughter in the whole wide world to help your mommy. Okay?"

I watch my mother walk to the door, then flick off the bedroom light.

"Look, I've left the light on in my bedroom. You'll be able to see if you want." She disappears down the hallway, the sound of her footsteps disappearing with her.

I reach over to the lamp but stop. I sniff and smell the scorch of Dragon flames. Quick, I hug my knees and smile at the light coming from my mother's bedroom.

Light is where Mommy is.

I listen to the sounds of leaving. The rustle of her coat. The tap of her shoes. The door shuts behind my mother. The lock clicks loud. The best daughter in the whole wide world lies with her eyes wide open and listens to the noises, picking apart the house-talking sounds from the Dragon sounds. The kiss on my forehead grows cold as the room fills with shadows that stalk and haunt.

Wasted Brains
by Jewel

Mom's quite smart about
doing dumb really well.

Once, she's talking to one of
her many possible husbands when
he asks how does she know so much?

Mom tucked her smarts so far
back inside her head, I think, she
forgot how smart she really is.

Mom believes most men act like they're
some chest-pounding,
vine-swinging hero,
but they're really fragile inside.
It's up to women to take care of
them, letting them
think they're doing all the decision-making.

Seems to me this
waste of a good brain
shows no respect for
either one.

Rule #2
Be careful what you care about

My mom's a soft-boiled egg in a hard-boiled world.

The day before my tenth birthday, my mom is being beaten. Again.

I'm afraid the possible daddy will not stop in time. I stand in the hall off the new foyer, hiding in the shadows, scared, unable to move my legs. My heart is as loud as the thuds in the other room.

From beside the stairway of the new-to-us house, I can see into the living room. My mother kneels on the floor, bent small to expose less of herself, and covers her head with her arms. The boyfriend's arms jackhammer on her like he's drilling her into the floor.

My mom screeches and says, "Just a birthday party. That's all."

"Who do you think you are, spending my money?" Spit flies with each word.

The boyfriend's shoulders curve inward and his head falls forward as he lets out a gush of disgust. He rolls his head on his neck to look up at the ceiling, like he's wondering why his life has to be so hard. He moves to one side as if he's done with her, then with a backhand sweeps across the table knocking over all the pictures and knickknacks. Picture frames crack, glass breaks, objects roll away.

My mom ducks, then sneaks a glimpse from under her hair. "She's ten. I wanted to do something nice."

The latest boyfriend feigns a step in her direction and laughs when my mom cringes and scrambles.

"Shit. Nice is you being able to do anything right. I needed that money. Had something to buy." He jabs his chest with his thumb. "What's nice going to buy me now, huh? How are you going to fix that, huh?"

He hits her, again. With his fist. Both fists. On her arms. On her back. On her head.

My body jerks with the thumps from his fist on her body. Will my mom die this time?

A cut over my mother's eye bleeds down her face. She's dying. So much blood.

I grab the phone, punch the three numbers, and relief comes with the voice. With my hand over the phone and my mouth, I whisper, "My mom needs help. Bad."

I take root with the phone in my hand. A tiny voice comes from the receiver, but I'm hypnotized and paralyzed. My brain refuses to take in any more.

The crashes, the bangs, and the grunts grow louder, then stop. The cries become fainter.

The latest boyfriend slouches on the sofa. "You think your shit register job makes enough for all of us. I have needs too. Not that you care." With one foot he kicks my mom each time she tries to get up off the floor.

Sirens reach the front of the house.

Near me, knocks sound loud on the door. From inside the living room, the boyfriend takes a break from beating my mom to yell, "What d'ya want?"

"It's the police. Open up."

He flips the foyer light on and opens the door. Two cops stand in the doorway.

"Sir, we'd like to make sure everyone is all right. May we come in?"

The latest catches me standing a few feet away under the shadows of the stairs next to the table with the phone. He takes a step at me and points. "You're the reason for all this trouble."

I try to swallow but my mouth is dry.

One of the cops moves between us, and they usher the boyfriend back into the living room.

From the living room, my mother's voice filled with sobs becomes a wail. "He didn't do anything."

The boyfriend's words come out loud like gunshots. "It's the kid's fault."

Cop voices, lower, quieter, bring calm. "Why don't you sit down?"

Help is here. Things will get better.

The cops walk the latest boyfriend out the door with his hands behind his back. My mom, crying and holding a blood-soaked cloth to her forehead, follows them out. Her purse is pinched between her arm and her body; the broken purse strap dangles behind her.

I want to grab the strap.

"What about her? She needs help," I tell the officers as they walk down the sidewalk, but no one answers me.

I shiver in the night air. It wasn't my fault. I told her to forget the birthday party. I told her she was birthday enough. The pain hatches in my stomach and grows into my body, follows each vein, causing the flames to lick at my skin so it hurts to be touched, and I want to be held so badly.

I follow the police officers down to the sidewalk, but they shut me out when they close the cruiser's door with my mother sitting inside. "A social worker will be here to get you in a few minutes. Wait inside the house for her. This officer will stay with you."

Taillights vanish around the corner. I go into the house with the smiling man, who spits out words meant to assure and calm.

I pick up a cushion and set it on my lap. With my finger, I circle a spot of my mother's blood. If she dies, I will, too.

"Why don't you tell me what happened tonight?" The police officer moves closer to study the picture of my mother hanging on the wall.

My mom's hurt, and I'm not with her. How will she remember that I love her? My breath stops, my heart aches, my brain hurts.

The police officer picks up a broken picture frame and puts it on the table.

I want to scream at him. Those are my mother's. Don't touch them. You have no right.

"You want to help your mother, don't you? If you tell me what happened, we'll be able to stop that guy from hurting your mom again." The police officer sits where my mother's boyfriend sat. He pulls out a notebook and gets ready to write.

"He didn't hurt you in any way, did he?"

I point to the kitchen. "I need a glass of water."

He nods approval and continues to talk. "Things appear bad for you right now, but don't you worry. By tomorrow, everything will be better. Kids nowadays are much tougher than when I was a boy."

I walk through the kitchen entrance, pass the glass rack, out the back door, and hitchhike to the hospital.

Mom needs me.

At the hospital, there's no Mom. Nobody's heard of her.

"Sorry, honey. We don't have anyone by that name. Have you tried the other hospitals?"

Without money for the phone, I thumb a lift to the police station. They have to tell me what they did with her. Don't they? She's my mother.

"You'll have to wait for all the paperwork to be filled out. Sit over there, and she'll be out in no time." The mustached man

behind the desk points to a grimy white plastic chair that's supposed to be curved for a person's butt. Not mine.

I whisper, "Evil spirits away with you. Only angels and good
fairies visit my mother tonight." I hope my mom, wherever she's
at, receives my message.

Hours climb, one on top of the other, each hour getting
longer than the one just done. Just when I think I'm going to take
shape with the chair, my mom comes out. I'm an hour old into
my birthday, and she's my present.

She has a white bandage on her forehead with a round red
circle in the middle of the gauze, like it's her passport out of hell.

She walks weary. Her eyes are dark all around. Her shoulders
curve with shame. With the broken strap dangling, she holds her
purse tight to her stomach, like it's a hot water bottle. I want to
help her carry the load. I gently put my arm around her waist and
walk beside her as she shuffles like a person just out of the hospital after the roof has fallen on them. But she bucks away when
she feels my arms.

The frazzle is gone now.

Her back goes soldier-sharp.

With a snap, she adjusts her rose-colored sweater draped
over her shoulder. The dainty, hand-stitched roses at the collar
stand out bright.

She squints at me with one swollen eye. "You called the
police?"

I nod. She loves me so much. Now she knows I love her the
same, too. "Wasn't nothing, I just . . ."

"I guess I'll never be able to trust you again."

Rule #3
Look both ways before crossing your life

As the latest boyfriend leaves, another one moves us to the south side of San Antonio. There we graduate to "Trailer Trash." In the new-to-us old trailer, the living room and kitchen are at one end, the master bedroom at the other. My room, without a lock on the door, is next to the bathroom in the middle.

The stove is covered in grease; the refrigerator rattles on and off. Our furniture's crammed in the living room, and the television, the newest boyfriend's contribution, is the biggest we've ever had.

A few weeks after we move, as I walk in from playing outside, I catch my mother hanging up the phone. She explains how we aren't able to feed another mouth. I look at her stomach and wonder.

The next week, after her visit to the clinic, my mother is singing. No more worries. The problem's gone. "Just like you could be," says my mother's latest boyfriend as he looks at me and winks with a big friendly smile on his face.

My mom pours him more coffee with her hand on his shoulder. "Isn't he just so friendly?"

Later that day in the hallway, my mother stands, poised, with the broken-strap-purse in her hand, the strap twisted around her arm like an Egyptian bracelet. "Jewel, do you want anything from the store?"

"Uh."

She sighs. "You're fourteen and a half, and I can't get a whole sentence out of you."

I remain quiet.

"Okay. I'll bring you some gum."

I lie on my bed and count the cracks on the ceiling. In my bedroom, the maple chest of drawers sits against the wall next to the door. Across the room by the window, the half-stripped student desk is piled high with schoolbooks. My mother painted my bed white but promises each time she enters the room that she will finish varnishing the desk the following weekend.

The door slams when my mother leaves. The television in the living room is cranked up so loud I can make out the word, "Jeopardy."

I should be doing my homework, but I count all the reasons against doing my assignments.

I'm on my twenty-seventh reason when a creak signals a step on the floor at the living-room end of the hallway. I sit up.

I stare at the door and picture the person approaching from the other side.

I draw my knees up to my chest and wrap my arms around my legs as the doorknob twists.

The door swings on its hinges. My mother's latest boyfriend stands there. "Caught me." Bill grins.

I place my chin on my knees and stare as if I were watching a spider creep up on its prey. He's not much taller than I am and has thick hair on his arms. His eyebrows twist up, and he squints because he needs glasses. He hikes up his pants and runs his hand inside of the waistband to adjust himself.

"C'mon. I was just kidding." He cruises into the room, his smile advancing his intentions. "I just thought you might want some company."

"I've got homework to do." I slip off the bed, step to my desk, and pick up my biology textbook. I turn and face him with the open book in my hands.

Evil spirits away with you. Only angels and good fairies visit me tonight, I chant in my head.

"Maybe I can help. It may surprise you, but I was a whiz at school."

"Yeah, it surprises me." Just stay cool. He'll go away. A frown crosses his face. "You're a real funny girl."

"That's what everyone says." I lean against the desk and pretend to read the book. Nothing is going to happen. I won't let it.

"You know what's wrong with you . . ." Bill leans into my space and subtracts inches from between us.

I turn a page of the book. He can't touch me. I'm protected. He can't touch me. The purple feather protects me.

" . . .You need to be taken down a peg. You're just too smart for your own good." He coils out a hand to touch my shoulder.

I twist away, pull out the chair, and plop into it. I grab a notebook, my hand sticking to the plastic cover, snap the binder open, and rip a page out. Don't look at him. He'll disappear.

Bill stands behind me and paws my hair. "We could make your mother happy if we got along better."

I shake my head. The heavy musk of his aftershave fogs the air around me as he leans over. I hold my breath determined not to breathe until he is gone.

"Your mother worries a lot about you. If you were happier, her life would be easier." He claws his fingers through my hair.

I copy words out of the biology book. Just pretend. Just pretend nothing is happening. Or going to happen.

He slips his hands over my shoulders and down the front of my blouse. I didn't ask for this. I know I didn't ask for this. I didn't do anything.

I jump up, push hard against his arms, then jerk away. "Leave me alone, you jerk." Act tough. Be tough. He can't touch me if I'm hard and bitter.

"C'mon, darling. All I want to do is play. You can't tell me you haven't done this before."

He moves closer and grinds his body against mine. I step backwards until I'm up against the dresser and he pins me there. "All those boys wouldn't be hanging around if they weren't getting their rocks off."

"If you touch me, I'll bust your balls." I stretch myself as large as I can be. Xena, the Warrior Princess, will kill you if you hurt me. The Hulk will pulverize you. Darth Vader will zap you, and Dracula will suck you dry.

He grabs me by the arm and yanks me to him. "All I want is what the others are getting. How come you're so stingy with me?"

"Because you stink." I struggle in his grip, trying to get loose. He can't hurt me. He can't hurt me. If I don't let him, he can't hurt me.

"Just one little kiss."

I kick him on the shins. My foot hurts. Hurts a lot. It's all right as long as he hurts, too.

"Ow!" He swings his arm and backhands me across the face, hanging onto me with his other hand.

I reel from the slap and taste blood at the corner of my mouth. My head aches, and my ears buzz. "Get away from me."

"You're just like your mother. Think you're worth more than you are. Well, I got something for you that can change all that." He flings me onto my bed and unhooks his belt.

I kick out at him with both legs as he looms over me. "Slimebag. I'll kill you." If I'm tough, he won't get me. If I'm strong, he won't do me.

"C'mon, darling, you'll enjoy it. You want me. I've seen the looks you've given me." He pins my legs down with his knees and catches my wrists in each hand.

I spit in his face. No way. No how. No matter. I'd rather die than let him touch me. "You lowlife trash."

He hauls back to hit me when the front doorknob jiggles from the key in the lock.

Bill bolts out of the room and cannonballs down the hallway as my mother steps through the doorway.

"What's happening, dear?"

She catches him as he hooks his belt tight. I pull myself together, then watch through the doorway.

"Just went to the bathroom. Whatsa matter? A man has to have permission to use the bathroom in this dump?"

"No. Of course not. It's just that . . ." My mother gulps. She puts a hand out to him but doesn't touch him.

He shoves by her on his way to the living room. "What?" Bill looms over my mother.

With my head down, I pass by them on my way to the kitchen.

My mother draws her hand back and covers her throat. "Nothing."

Bill asks, "Why're you back?" as he sits down on the recliner and reaches for the television remote.

"I forgot the money." My mother moves to the bookshelf, grabs an old coffee can wrapped in my second-grade drawing, and dips her hand inside. She pulls out a couple of dollar bills. "Oh, I thought there was more." She sniffs, eyes tearing.

Bill sticks his hand in his pocket. "Here. Here's some money. Never met a person that's so lousy at hanging onto their money. Stop that sniffling. Don't go blubbering on me. I can't stand a crying woman."

I walk by, holding a cold soda against my cheek. Without glancing at either of them, I say, "Last of the big-time spenders."

I go down the hallway to my room. Stupid moron. Stupid, stupid jerk. Mom knows better. Mom will get him.

"Kid's good for nothing," Bill spits out.

My mom takes the money and follows me down the hallway.

"Where are you going?" Bill yells at her.

She stops and looks back. "Just checking up on my baby."

"What for? The brat's spoiled enough." Bill turns up the television. "Just plays her radio too loud."

"I'll tell her to turn it down." She walks down the hallway.

"Doesn't do no good. Kid don't listen to nothing from nobody. She's nothing but trouble. Lies about everything."

My mother speaks from the doorway of my bedroom. "Honey, can you turn the volume down a little? It bothers Bill."

I'm at my desk with my back to the door. I reach across my books to turn the radio knob. I return to my books. *Come closer, Mom. Come and take a look at me.*

"Is everything okay?"

I answer from behind a veil of hair that falls around my face, "Yeah, why wouldn't it be?" *Just look at me, Mom. Really look at me. Just love me. Really love me.*

"I just thought . . ."

"Mom, go to the store, or supper will be late, and that jerk will have something else to bitch about." *Take care of me first. Love me first, Mom.*

"Honey, I wish you would try to get along with him. Bill's being very nice to me. After the wedding, everything will return to normal."

"If you say so, Mom."

"Honey, a fourteen-year-old has no way of understanding how hard life can actually be."

I can feel my mother reach out a hand, hesitate, then draw her hand back.

She retreats down the hallway. "I'll be back in a few minutes."

After the front door shuts behind her, Bill fills the doorway to my bedroom. "Say a word, your mother's dead."

I stand and face him. The left side of my face is bruised, my lip cut. "You ever touch me again, I'll kill you."

We stare, threats telegraphed in both directions. Bill charges into the room and stops short when I stand up, push the chair away with the back of my legs, and pull the butcher knife from under the notebook.

"See this? It's yours for good if you ever come near me again." I point with my chin toward the bed. "I'm sleeping with this knife under my pillow, too."

Bill spins away and walks down the hallway. "Just like her mother. Stupid."

"Don't forget. Just in case you walk in your sleep," I yell after him.

I can do this. I can do this alone.

I close the bedroom door and stand in front of the mirror. I can do this by myself. I grab a chunk of hair and hold it up in the air, away from me. I slide the butcher knife across the hair, and the strands hang from my hand. Sawing the knife, I hack another handful of hair.

Chunk by chunk.

If I'm ugly, they'll leave me alone.

Wasted Inches
by Jewel

Seems funny how five, more or less, inches
of flesh can make some people feel so superior.
You'd think someone could map out a way for
people to talk with each other without
guys having to plug their thing in.

They must figure women are just around
for plugging into; why else have the hole?

People gossip about how good
plugging the hole feels,
while actually feeling nothing.
They think doing the inches proves
they're wanted and lovable.

Some people measure affection in inches.

Rule #4
Trust what you see today; you may want it to disappear tomorrow

My mom, her newest latest boyfriend, and I move into a sprawling brick house on the Northside. Bunches of flowers stand in tall vases on tabletops around the living room. The floor polish and lemon cleaner attacks your nose when you enter a room. The smell of off-the-floor store-bought furniture wars with the pot-pourri pots scattered across the room. Lucy Blake-Elahi's painting covers one wall where you can view it when you walk in. Angela believes artwork makes her house sophisticated.

My room has a lock on the door.

My mom rises from the sofa when I step into the house. "Honey, can you come in here?" She's tidy in a blue, sleeveless, wraparound dress that shows off her small waist.

"What do you want?" I stop in the entryway to the living room, letting my backpack slide to the floor. I check out the person who stands next to my mother.

"This is Mrs. Clarke, Jewel." Mom moves across the living room and stops next to me. She starts to wrap an arm around my shoulders.

I step back, pulling away from her. Must be a special guest if she wants to play the happy-mother-and-daughter routine.

My mom stretches a weak smile across her face. "She's a social worker."

I look from the social worker to her. "Yeah, what's it to me?"

21

The woman motions. "Why don't you sit down, so we can discuss what's happening?"

Instead, I lean against the wall and stare at the woman. They can think I'm dumb, but I won't be led into their games that easily.

The stranger is a head taller than Mom. The woman's black hair is combed back from her face; light brown eyes and a big smile show her willingness to be friendly. Her straight black skirt and jacket conceals any curves. I wonder what else it hides.

I never take my eyes from the social worker. "What's going on? What're you doing here?"

Mom turns to the social worker and cries, "You see? This is what I'm talking about." She covers her face with her hands.

Mrs. Clarke unlocks eye contact with me, then speaks to Mom. "Why don't you take a seat, Angela. I'm sure if Jewel wants to sit, she will when she's ready."

My mom hurries across the room. She never moves that fast except when she wants something.

Mrs. Clarke watches her settle in, then says to me, "I gather you weren't warned about my coming."

I sigh, a long bored breath, and turn my head toward the kitchen doorway. They can talk all they want. I'm not getting into any of this.

Mom reports, "Since she was fourteen, I haven't been able to control her. She doesn't listen to me. I never know where she is."

Mrs. Clarke nods. "That's all in the report. I'm interested to hear what Jewel has to say."

I fold my arms, lean my shoulder against the wall, and cross one ankle over the other foot.

"She's in her room all day," Mom interrupts again. "She never comes out. Never talks with anyone. I don't even know if she has any friends."

Mrs. Clarke shifts on the sofa and faces Mom. "I thought you said she was always out, you never know where she is?"

Eyes wide, my mom covers her mouth with her hand.

I have to give her credit. She tries. She really does.

"I mean, well, sometimes I check her room, and she's not there." Mom lays one hand on top of the other on her lap.

"Do you ask Jewel where she's been?" Mrs. Clarke studies her.

"Of course I do. I'm a good mother. Nowadays things are harder. I'm not here to supervise all her comings and goings. I have to have a job because I want my daughter to have nice things."

I curtsy and make a fashion model turn so Mrs. Clarke can take note of the color-coordinated cotton T-shirt, emblazoned with "I make boys cry," and designer jeans with a jean jacket. They want smart; they'll get smart. Nobody talks about me without getting something back.

Mrs. Clarke smiles. "I'm sure you do the best you can."

I cover a bored yawn with a hand and lean against the wall. I still don't have a clue as to where this is going. I doubt even my mother realizes what she's doing.

My mom searches inside a shiny, new purse with a stiff upright handle.

Well. Things are good on the home front. One of her latest boyfriends finally bought her something.

From inside the new purse, she pulls out a tissue and dabs at her eyes. "I love my daughter very much." She peeks over the tissue. "This pains me so. But I just can't cope with her constant disruptions. Shoplifting, skipping school, fighting."

A chair in the kitchen scrapes against the floor. Must be the latest boyfriend.

"You do understand, don't you?" My mom cocks her head and dabs at her eyes again.

Mom's a pro all right. Down to the sniffling. She has victim down pat.

"Angela, we're not passing judgment on you," Mrs. Clarke says.

"I don't really want to do this. I love her very much. But I have a life to lead. I just can't take care of her and myself too." I look into the kitchen to ignore my mom's woes.

"Jewel, do you have anything to add?" Mrs. Clarke asks.

Through the kitchen doorway, I spot mom's latest boyfriend as he leans his butt against the stove. His white starched shirt, which I ironed, is wrinkled from a day of fast-talking sales, and his red striped necktie is still knotted tight at the throat. With his finger sticking straight out and his thumb in the air, he aims his finger gun at me, smiling the whole while. Bang. I'm dead.

Without taking my eyes off the man, I ask, "You getting married, Mom?"

My mom fidgets in her seat. "I was going to tell you. I was. But you've been so hard to talk to lately, I just couldn't . . ." She grips the arm of the sofa; her knuckles bleach.

Mom's boyfriend nods. Should have guessed. Third marriage be the magic number?

"Am I invited to the wedding, Mom?"

He points at me, then thrusts his thumb out toward the back door. I'm gone. History. He stays. For how long is the question. He doesn't know. I's always the one left to pick up the pieces when the likes of him abandon my mother.

"You going to wear a white gown?" I watch the latest.

Mrs. Clarke twists around to look through the doorway, but she can't see into the kitchen from where she sits. "Jewel?"

I pick up my backpack and sling it over my shoulder. "I'll go pack." To the kitchen doorway, I add, "What do I care?"

He's just one of many. I's the one who's always there in the end.

"Your suitcase is right over there." My mom jumps in, then covers her mouth. She rushes to add, "I mean, I wanted to make sure you had all your nice clothes and that everything was packed nice. So you wouldn't ruin anything." She smiles at Mrs. Clarke. "Teenagers. They have no sense of what things cost." Her worth is all tied up in her appearance, in her things, and in how I look. My mom takes care to color inside each lie.

I gawk at her, then turn slowly toward the kitchen. My mom packed my stuff? This latest promises my mom marriage only if she gets rid of me.

From the kitchen, the boyfriend clasps his hands over his head in victory.

Round one goes to him. Loser. But he won't be here for long. Latests never are. I's the one my mom really loves. No matter if he marries her or not.

"What the heck. Like I care about any of this." I turn and head for the door.

My mom jumps to her feet. "Honey, please, I'll miss you so much."

I take another step. I'll be back fast enough when my mom needs me.

"Baby, you have to understand. This is so difficult for me." My mother wipes tears from her eyes as she stands with her arms open wide for a hug.

I stop and turn around. Difficult on her? Tough on me. Cruel on both of us.

"I've always loved you best." My mom stretches her arms out to me.

I jerk my chin in the direction of the kitchen. "Right, but you like their paychecks more."

The man nods and smiles.

He promised to pay me back for saying no. In the end, I'll be back before the scent of his aftershave is out of the bathroom.

My mom presses her hand over her heart as if it hurts. "It's a hard world."

"So you tell me."

If she had ever bothered to notice, she'd know I found that out a long time ago. A really long time ago.

My mom sinks onto the sofa like a tire losing air. "Baby, when you were little, you'd be next to me, talking a mile a minute. Everyone thought you were so darling when you'd speak in your cute little girl way."

I roll my eyes. Oh, spare me the children stories.

"How this be for darling? I'm getting the heck out of here." I spin on my heels, walk out the front, and shut the door carefully.

Wasted Colors
by Jewel

My mom's like a box of crayons.

Too much heat, a crayon melts.
Squeeze a crayon too hard, it snaps.

The latest determines what color she likes.

Her worth is all tied up in her appearance,
in her things, and in how I look.

She takes care to color inside each lie.

In my mom's box of crayons,
I'm the piece that won't fit.

I'm the throwaway piece.

Rule #5
Listen to how people do; promises are just words

"If there was ever a girl that stretched people's limits, it's you, Jewel. The Butlers were lovely people." Mrs. Clarke drops Jewel's suitcase into her trunk with a loud thud.

From her mother's house she went into emergency care for a day, then into her first foster home. After a couple of weeks of isolating herself in her assigned room, she's being moved into a new foster home.

Jewel skips around the back of the social worker's red car and sits in the passenger seat. She beams at the social worker as she slides into the driver's seat and says, "Why it be just me? They does stuff, too. I just being my high self-esteem self."

"Well, the Luddingtons are wonderful people. I've told them about you, and they're happy to have you. I'm sure you'll like them." The social worker shuts the car door and buckles her seat belt. "They're first-time foster parents. Please, be nice to them."

"I nicest to all persons. All time friendly and helpful. Like a Girl Scout." For a salute, Jewel sticks three fingers in the air next to her forehead.

She grins, stretching muscles she hasn't used in a long time. This could be fun, she thinks.

The social worker turns the key in the ignition. "When are you going to stop speaking like that? People won't take you seriously if you continue to speak with that Jewel Speak."

"When my mother takes me home, I'll go back to sounding like my mother's proper daughter." Jewel flips her hand out in front of her. "Until she be coming for me, I talking so fine. Just like I pleasing."

"Jewel, this situation is a lot more complicated than . . ." The social worker explores Jewel's face. Jewel dazzles the woman with her most serious expression, and the social worker sighs. "Put on your seat belt."

"Ah, yes. Most importantly keeping foster child safest."

Rule #6
Grown-ups are smart except when it comes to kids

A few weeks later, Jewel and the social worker go to court.
The system needs to tidy up their paperwork and brand her with
a label.

On the way to the courthouse, Mrs. Clarke explains the court
proceedings. "First, your lawyer and the guardian *ad litem* will
explain your situation to the judge. This is to turn custody over to
the State, so we can continue supervising your care. The State's
lawyer will describe your behavior and make the recommenda-
tion that you be officially placed in foster care."

This time Mrs. Clarke's outfit, a straight skirt and matching
jacket, is blue. The blouse is a paler blue. Jewel wonders how
many color versions of the identical outfit this woman has. "Will
I goes up there and be asked questions?"

Mrs. Clarke glances over. "You plan on speaking like that to
the judge?"

Jewel slumps against the car door. "I in trouble if I open my
mouth or keep my lips shut."

"Your mother isn't around for you to impress with your
games."

Jewel innocently opens her eyes. "You the sister of Freud?"

"You'll have to stop talking this way when you're in school.
The students won't appreciate your weird language."

"Soooo? I got to speak?"

Mrs. Clarke shoots in front of another car. "You won't have to testify, but the judge may ask you some questions. You can answer from your seat."

Jewel grins. "What happening with you?"

The social worker frowns at Jewel. "You'll stay on my case-load, in a foster home under my supervision."

"You play fairy godmother on me. Oh, puhleeeze!"

"Are you going to make me wrong before I even start?" Mrs. Clarke checks the traffic and glances at Jewel as she makes a turn. "If you'll let me, we can be friends, Jewel." The blinker clicks off loudly after she completes the turn.

She hardly knows Jewel, and already the social worker's offering to be her friend. Jewel has but one friend. Only one. Her mother. That's all she needs. Or wants. She'll show this social worker how it is. Jewel shouts, "Watch out."

Jewel hangs onto the handle of the door as the social worker swerves to the left. The woman glides the car into an open space at the curb and stares hard at Jewel, like she's reading her brain.

Jewel smiles. "I guess I imagining I see something in the street, like you imagining about my mom. This temporary. Until my mom back on her feet. My mom forced into doing what she done." Jewel crosses her arms. "You seeing. She coming back for me real soon."

They reach the court building and rock into a parking space. Jewel steps out of the car. The parking lot reflects back at her from the mirrored front of the tallest building.

Mrs. Clarke moves ahead of Jewel. "Let's go. We don't have much time."

Jewel takes a step to follow Mrs. Clarke, but then stops and gawks at her shoeless foot. "Hey! My shoe is gone!"

The social worker turns back and covers her mouth laughing.

Jewel hops backwards and slips her foot back into her high top with no shoelaces. She yanks her foot so the rubber sole that melted onto the pavement rips up. "This Texas sun trying to steal my sneaker. I want to make a report."

The social worker chuckles and says, "I know you don't want to go in but . . ."

The nasty face she gives the woman only brings more laughter. They walk up to the building and enter through the front entrance. The refrigerated air blasts them with a whoosh.

Jewel cranes her neck to eyeball all the different hallways that extend from the front door. "Well, when I get the chair, at least I get fried in air-condition."

The social worker walks to the elevators without a peek at her. Jewel burps. Either the social worker's become really good at not listening to Jewel, or Jewel has to get funnier. She follows the woman into the elevator.

"Hey, you got a name that goes with other stuff. Social morker. Social lacker." She grins.

The social worker ignores her.

On the third floor, they turn left, follow the corridor, and enter a small room with green walls the color of a soldier's uniform. At one end of a long table sits a man in a white shirt, red tie, and navy blue slacks. The matching suit jacket hangs over the back of the chair. His black suspenders have yellow smiley faces in a row down the straps. His files and papers are stacked in a lopsided pile in front of him. His eyes skim over them, assessing, then he grins. The lawyer has the face of a baby boy.

"You finally arrived." He checks his wristwatch, then the wall clock. "Sit down. Sit down. We have a lot to talk about and very little time."

Jewel sits at the farthest end of the table and watches the social worker as she slips out her one file from a portfolio, opens it, and aligns the file perfectly against the table's edge beside the lawyer's jumble of paperwork. She sets the portfolio to the side, unbuttons her jacket, and lets it flap open so her blouse shows.

Jewel is so surprised, her mouth drops open. This is the first sign of relaxing she's ever spotted on the tight-knotted social rocker.

The social worker folds her hands over her organized file and addresses the lawyer in crisp words. "This appears to be an easy case. I don't believe there is much need for preamble."

The lawyer boy glances up at the social worker, then swings his gaze over to Jewel. "I want to get acquainted with my client a bit more personally than just meeting in the doorway of the courtroom and spouting off to the judge what I read in the report. How about it, Jewel? Let's get to know each other."

Jewel sticks a finger up her nose and scratches her butt with the other hand.

The lawyer boy smiles like a lightbulb has been turned on inside his face. "Ah, I'm prepared for you." He scrambles through his paperwork and pulls out a thick paperback. *Born to Win*. He raises the book so they can see the cover. "I've read this cover to cover and anything a kid can throw at me, I'm ready."

The social corker wipes the corner of her mouth with her finger to cover the smile popping out. "Yes, however, this case is a simple one. We need to have Jewel mandated into custody care as soon as possible. I have a placement ready for her."

The lawyer boy winks at Jewel. "Have you had a chance to examine this placement Mrs. Clarke is referring to?"

"Who this Mrs. Clarke? Someone that gives a flying . . ."

With eyes on the lawyer boy, the social wrecker raises her hand shoulder high, lowers her arm, and places her hand flat on the table. Noiselessly.

". . . about me." Darn, the woman doesn't even make a sound. Didn't even glance her way. Her mom would have screamed, or turned to the lawyer boy to fix Jewel, acting all helpless. This social worker is an all-contained, self-sealed bundle. The woman continues to talk, but Jewel understands what's expected of her.

"The children rarely have a choice in where they go."

The lawyer boy has never learned his manners. He interrupts.

"Yes, but . . ."

"Foster parents are scrutinized when they apply and well trained if selected."

Oh, oh. The lawyer boy draws the wrath of Social Worker Wisdom and Education onto his head.

"Not many people volunteer for these placements, so . . ."

"Yes, yes, I've read the statistics, but tests have proven if the kids . . ."

"I not a kid." Jewel shoots him her nastiest glare.

"Right, excuse me, young lady." He nods in her direction. "If these young people were more involved in the decisions regarding their situations, there would be fewer runaways and less trouble with their placement."

"I assure you," Mrs. Clarke's words shoot out like rockets, "I will give Jewel every opportunity to scrutinize her placement before tossing her into some hovel."

The lawyer boy nods, like one of those bobbing toys without catching on that the social blaster is blasting him with her words.

"Good. Good. Now for the facts of the case. The mother is unfit to function as a parent?" He nods toward the social worker.

"The mother feels unable to deal with the strains put on her by Jewel's disruptive behavior." Mrs. Clarke corrects him.

The lawyer boy blinks at Jewel. "Well, I think you've been very cooperative in this meeting."

Jewel crosses her eyes, tilts her head, and lets her tongue hang, pushing out spit so drool slides down her chin.

The social worker hides her chuckle by readjusting her file. "Sir, you have to understand the dynamics at play."

"Oh, but I do, I do." The lawyer boy holds up his *Born to Win* paperback.

"Excuse me, that's a fine book for parents and people who have to deal with children. With Jewel, this matter runs a bit deeper."

Jewel groans. Loudly. Here comes the dissecting part, picking her apart, theory by theory.

"A pattern of denial exists between the mother and the child. An agreement of sorts."

"Of course, of course." The lawyer boy nods as he thumbs through other files.

"Jewel has performed the role of protector and guardian for her mother. Parentification."

Wow, this social worker has her fighting weight. She stops this lawyer boy cold in his syllables. Jewel doesn't remember a time her mom has ever been able to do the same thing with any of her latest boyfriends or husbands. Jewel wishes her mom could learn how this social worker does it.

No.

Wait.

Her mom's fine. Super fine as she is. This one dices, slices, and grates on your nerves, folks, all for the price of an education. Call the 800 number and get one of your very own social bonkers.

"Jewel's sense of responsibility has been exploited."

The lawyer boy picks up the paperback, licks his fingertips, and flips through the pages. "Oh, yes, I read that part. Chapter twelve, I think. Good discussion. Good explanation. I understand what you mean exactly."

The social cheeker sucks her cheek in, and Jewel flinches as the woman chomps the inside of her mouth. Ouch! Must have hurt bad.

The social worker-turned-Warrior Princess closes the file. She folds her hands over the file, then leans her body forward. The arrow is in the bow and leveled at the lawyer boy. He'll be spread out on the floor before he's fully aware he's been shot.

"This is the one role Jewel will never be adept at filling." The Warrior Princess pierces the face of the lawyer boy with an intensity Jewel has never seen on anyone before.

The lawyer boy nods again as he reads a file.

The Warrior Princess slaps one hand on the file he's browsing. Lawyer boy scans their faces. "Yes, yes, yes." He closes his file on her hand. "The defense mechanisms have been discussed and theorized by experts . . ."

Jewel scrapes the chair across the floor as she stands. The sound is quite loud in this mostly empty room. Empty with the souls of the likes of her. Both of them turn to her.

"Done twisting my brain noddles into itty bitty knots? What you think? I not feel? I not understand?"

Jewel walks around toward the other end of the table and stands near the social worker. "My mom loves me. She be back for me. You and all your swanky words and your thick books." She picks up the lawyer boy's bible and drops the paperbook on the table with a loud thump. "You get nothing about what my mom wants for me or thinks for me. You spouting off words with no heart in them. This what you call knowing me. Talking like I not even in the room."

Jewel leans over the table, and with a backward swing of her arm, she swipes all the lawyer boy's paperwork off the table onto the floor.

The baby-faced lawyer jumps out of his chair like he has been splashed. "Oh my goodness. My files." He falls to his knees, picks up papers, and clutches them to his chest.

The social worker stands and puts a hand on Jewel's shoulder.

Jewel shrugs her off and walks out of the room.

"We'll wait for you in the corridor," the social worker says as she follows Jewel out the door.

Mrs. Clarke doesn't scold her about what she did or tell her how she's been bad. She actually backs Jewel up. Something her mom has never done. But this doesn't make any difference. Her mom is special, more special than this straight-back, head-held-high social worker walking next to her. She won't be tricked by this social worker acting like she cares.

"San Antonio Juvenile Court System. All rise."

A woman in a black robe enters the room.

"The Honorable Judge García presiding."

The judge sits down; everyone else sits down. The courtroom spectators are clustered in twos and threes, everybody keeping as much distance as they can from one another.

At a table in front of the banister, Jewel sits next to the lawyer boy, who moves his stack of files away from her reach. The lawyer representing the State stands at another table. The State's lawyer must think he looks mighty fine in a navy blue suit, starched white shirt, and narrow tie, his hair clipped short so the pink of his scalp shines. She wonders if he has smiley-faced suspenders, too. The social worker sits in the pew behind Jewel, on guard so she doesn't escape.

Jewel listens to the lawyers throw words up at the judge. The lawyer boy sticks a lot of labels like unmanageable and incorrigible on her like she's some dartboard. She wonders why the lawyer boy acts like everyone doesn't already know what's going to happen.

The State's lawyer uses words like undisciplined and disruptive. He mentions skipping school, out late at night, and shoplifting. She hears herself in the lawyers' talk. She slouches in the chair and works hard at looking bored. She's in good hands now.

When they leave the courtroom, the lawyer boy beams at her. "I think that went very well. I'm sure everything is going to work out beautifully for you from here on out."

Jewel takes one step in his direction; he straightens his tie and swallows. She speaks to the social worker while holding the lawyer boy's stare, "I got to pee. I trusted to do the bathroom thing on my own? Or you got to go, holding my hand like a fairy godmother?"

The social pointer points. "It's in that direction."

Jewel sashays over to the door. She looks back at the lawyer boy and the social princess and winks before she enters.

Wasted System
by Jewel

What is there to say

about a system

full of people

who are given

a bunch of needy kids?

Way too many duties,

little money,

for the hours

in one day,

expecting them to

perform miracles.

Yeah, I'm in good hands now.

Rule #7
Never unpack everything

The social worker sighs as she drops Jewel's suitcase into the trunk of the red car again. "Jewel. Why?"

"They asking if my mother ignorant white trash, or I mentally damaged for verbalizing like I does."

Wasted Mouth
by Jewel

My mouth, I'm told, is way too smart.
This is a confusing thought.
Grown-ups preach all the time for me to
get smart,
act smart,
think smart.
Except when they don't like
what comes out of my mouth,
they call me being too smart.

They shake their heads and predict
how my smart mouth is going to
head me directly into trouble.

Rule #8
Birthdays are for getting older, not wiser

The marriage and the brick house disappear within two months after I enter foster care. My mom rents a duplex with two bedrooms. She's waiting for me to come home.

I arrive straight from my last class. She has me take a scented bath with candles, then makes up my face and plays with my hair, trying to make it look nice. Then surprises me with a beautiful dress.

That evening we make popcorn.

"It's so great that you can spend the night. We'll be able to celebrate your birthday all night long, Jewel."

My mom smiles and slants her head down and asks in a girlfriend tone of voice, "Sweet sixteen. Have you ever been kissed? C'mon, you can tell me."

"Mom, why are we in these outfits? This dress is uncomfortable." I tug at the bodice to cover up what is popping out of the strapless bra my mom has made me put on.

"Gown, honey. It's an evening gown. Something special for a special girl. I like getting all dressed up."

She wears a red-sequined gown that is slicked against her body. I'm in a green dress with off-the-shoulder sleeves and a slit on the side, up to mid-thigh.

"I don't know why we had to get dressed up for pizza and popcorn."

"Listen, the cracking is all done. Take the popcorn out of the microwave and I'll get the bowl."

As I pull the bag open by its opposite corners, she holds ready a big plastic bowl. I pour the popcorn into the container. My mom says, "We got your favorite movie. *Night of the Living Dead.* "We?" I dump the empty package into the wastebasket under the sink.

"We. You and me against the world."

My mom grabs me by the waist and we dance around the room. I scoop out a smaller bowl of popcorn and feed a kernel to her. She takes a popcorn kernel and feeds it to me mama-bird-style while still dancing.

"You and me against the world."

I twirl in the center of the room, following my mother as she dances around me. I feed her another popcorn.

"Are those all the words you know of that song?"

"They're the only ones that count."

She pitches a popcorn at me. I bend and sway to catch the popcorn as it lands near my nose.

She smiles and tosses another kernel for me to catch. It hits my cheek and falls to the floor. I toss one to her and she bites on it midair. I giggle and toss two more in fast succession. She chews on one and lets the other fall to the floor; then laughing, she lobs three in a row. I come back with three more. We throw handfuls of popcorn at each other, laughing. I grab another bowlful as my mom stuffs my mouth with popcorn, then the food fight resumes. As I run out of ammunition, I hold up my hands to shield from the popcorn she is hurling by the handful.

From the doorway comes a voice. "Hey, what's going on here?"

Popcorn covers the floor. My mom and I stop instantly. I turn and check out the tall man in the doorway. He wears a dark suit with a red tie and is holding a pizza.

"I rang the doorbell but no one heard me, so I came in with the key you gave me." He dangles the key chain from his hand shoulder high.

My mom smiles. "That's why I gave it to you."

She moves toward the tall man and wraps both arms around his waist and leans her head on his chest. "Jewel, this is Adam."

"Whoa, watch it, little lady. Don't tip over the pizza."

She steps back. "Here, let me take it. Wasn't that nice of him to get us the pizza. What kind is it? Tomato and bacon with extra cheese?"

The man looks confused and shakes his head. "No, I got our favorite. Pepperoni." He looks at me and smiles. "I figured you'd want *our* favorite."

She smiles, avoiding my intent stare. "Of course, baby. You got it right. You always do. And the video?"

"Instead of the one you told me, I found that romantic comedy I mentioned the other night and you said you wanted to see." He holds up the video case in his hand and swings it side to side.

"Oh, how nice." My mom looks at me with intent in her eyes. "Right, Jewel? We always enjoy that kind of movie."

My shoulders cave in. "Yeah. Anything you say." I reach for the broom, but the tall man takes my hand.

"I must say you are beautiful. Angela, your sister is the spittin' image of you. Your mother must have been a beautiful woman."

Having heard this version before, I pull my hand away and snap the broom off its catch from the back of the pantry door.

"Oh, for heaven's sake. Put that away." The tall man grabs the broom from my grasp. "It's your birthday. You shouldn't have to do any chores." He looks at my mom and winks. "You two take the pizza into the living room, get the movie going, and settle yourselves in. I'll clean this up and be right there."

She takes the broom from Adam. "Oh no, my man won't be doing any sweeping. Not while I'm standing."

"Well, then, I'll hold the dustpan. Jewel, take the pizza, plates, and movie into the living room. We'll continue your birthday party in there."

As I slip the video into the player, I hear them laughing in the kitchen. I place three paper plates out with a slice of pizza in each. Then the movie starring someone called Audrey Hepburn comes on.

My mother and her latest enter the living room, holding hands. "Oh, good. The movie's started." Adam sits in the opposite corner of the sofa and she curls up against him.

A half hour later and only Adam's pizza is gone. I keep my eyes on the television set as my mom kisses Adam.

As the kissing grows in frenzy, I stand up and take the pizza into the kitchen and put it into the refrigerator.

She calls out from the living room. "Sweetheart?"

Adam smiles. "Yes."

She playfully slaps him on the chest. "Not you. My other sweetheart."

I stand in the entryway from the kitchen. "Yeah?"

"What are you doing? Aren't you going to finish the movie?"

I stare down at the floor. "No, I'm tired. I'm going to my room."

"Ah, honey, I wanted this to be fun for you." My mom pouts.

"It was . . . It is. I'm just tired. Okay?"

She stands next to the coffee table. "Well, of course, baby. If you're tired, but . . ."

I look up at my mom, sensing what is coming.

"If you're going to your room, Adam and I are going out. Okay? Since I'm dressed up and all. You won't mind, will you, sweetheart?"

Adam says, "Yes."

My mom laughs as she looks down on Adam. "Oh, you dear sweet man." She looks back up at me and moves to touch my forehead. "You're not getting sick, are you?"

I pull away and go around my mother to go to my room.

Adam yells out. "Good night, and you're welcome for the pizza."

I keep walking.

Adam looks at my mom. "Your sister's one very ungrateful young lady."

Rule #9
Find where the toilet paper is kept

The social worker parks in front of the townhouse. "This is a good place. I expect you to be on your best behavior."

Jewel rolls her eyes. "Yeah, they being the nicest people ever."

At the front door, the foster parents say hello to Mrs. Clarke and smile at Jewel. "Mr. Halupka, Mrs. Halupka. This is Jewel."

Jewel shakes their hands. The foster mother pats her hand. The foster father reaches to take her bag. She pulls the handle away and walks right by him a few steps and stops to wait for the social worker.

The social worker trails after the foster mom to inspect what's going to be Jewel's bedroom. "Oh, Jewel, how lovely. Your own bedroom. With your own bathroom. What do you think?"

"I need doing the toilet." Jewel smiles at the glowing foster parents and the frowning social worker. She turns and sashays into the bathroom.

The bathroom is pretty like the bedroom. The pale blues and yellow are soothing. A scented deodorant is plugged in somewhere because the ocean breeze is working hard to convince her to relax.

When she's done, she grabs for the toilet paper. The roll is out. From where she's sitting, she can't spot where they store the extra rolls. She's in a mess.

Afterwards, she catches up with the grown-ups downstairs. All of them are in the living room being serious. The social worker distributes informational brochures in case they have an emergency.

"Everything all right?" the foster mother asks.

Jewel nods ever so politely.

She learned a secret.

At this foster mother's house, the fancy dolls with round, crochet skirts hide a roll of toilet paper underneath their skirts.

Rule #10
What you wear is what they see

Jewel's shopping at a corner store, and the shopkeeper tracks her every move. She can guess what he thinks. She's a kid. She dresses like a punk. She must be bad.

She snatches a bunch of magazines off the shelf. She sniffs her armpits, makes a face, and tucks the magazines under her arm. She grabs three pops from the cooler. The shopkeeper taps his fingers on a shelf because he's sure she will be trouble.

She scuffs up to the cash register, moving slow, keeping eye contact with the shopkeeper. He slips behind the counter.

She's out the door. She hits the pavement. Feet smack greedily.

He runs after her, but he's too slow. She's laughing at the fool . . .

Cops race to the rescue.

Not hers.

Wasted Questions
by Jewel

The cops drop me onto a chair
and throw words at me.
They ask questions
but really don't want the answers.
They have me all figured out.

If I speak smart words,
that would make me something
different than what they expect.
They wouldn't know how to label me.

Words are what my mom strings together
all day long. One word after another,
blinking like Christmas decorations.
She believes if she can string enough
words together, she'll make our
life sunshiny like she wants the world to be.

My mom builds walls with her words
hoping to hide the pain.
Razzle, dazzle you with words; then you
won't know how the other hand hurts.

Words are what grown-ups use to
trap you, so you're accountable
for all they've done for you.
They toss out words like grenades,
regardless of the hurt left behind.

I have a lot of words in my head; that's
where they'll stay. I don't want them
stuffed inside like prisoners, but no
one has ever asked me to let them out.

Grown-ups insist that they
try to communicate with their teens,
they do ask questions.
Questions designed to draw out
the words inside someone's heart,
questions designed to force
out the words grown-ups want to hear.

These are the questions that come at you,
the questions that put you into a box the
person asking the question feels comfortable with.
Wasted questions that don't let me speak.

Rule #11
Show fear, and they rush to kill you

Jewel sits in a jail cell. Cold seeps up through the bottom of her sneakers, crawls right into her bones. She holds her body still so the shivering doesn't show.

It's not too swift to show fear in this place.

The light from overhead doesn't make it any sweeter, but a person can watch her back. The walls are grimy from bodies and despair rubbing against them. The floor is footprint dirty, and the smell of puke comes from the corners. Between the packed body and the peeing in the one toilet, your nose shuts down.

The temperature is set low. People shiver in little balls, attempting to stay warm and hold in their fear. Cold is one of the tricks the jailers use to make the inmates so uncomfortable they won't want to come back.

A big girl with dirty blonde hair comes up to Jewel and puts her cigarette in Jewel's face. "Want a puff?"

Jewel shakes her head as she stands up. The girl is not moving away.

"You turn me down, I get offended. I get offended, I do damage." She uses her body to shove into Jewel's space.

"Give it your best shot." Jewel digs in and pushes back as hard as she can. The air between them compresses as if they're squashing a balloon with their bodies.

"You calling me out?"

"Uh-uh."

"Then what?"

"You hitting me, I die killing you."

The big girl laughs really loud, then struts off to join her pack at the other corner of the cell.

They laugh. A few of them look Jewel over, nodding their heads, as if she's something they found under their shoe.

It doesn't matter to Jewel. She turns all the noise into a buzz. The buzz in her head keeps the ugly faces away.

Most times.

In the jail cell, with Jewel's head full of thoughts, the voice cuts right through the buzz. Jewel keeps her eyes closed. The voice calls Jewel's name again, and she gets up.

The smoker and her friends saunter over. They stand right in Jewel's path, as if nothing ever scares them.

Mrs. Clarke steps into the cell and stands in front of Jewel, the social worker's back to the smoker.

"You're the slowest girl I've ever known. Can't you get moving?"

She jabs Jewel's shoulder. The others back off.

In the social worker's red car, she throws words at Jewel. Right and left punches. Words like responsibility, dependability, accountability. She spits them out so fast; she says a few new ones.

Then Jewel catches the familiar ones.

"The Swinfords refuse to be involved in incidents of this kind. Skipping school and shoplifting is not the way to get ahead in the world. This could have worked out for you. But not any more. They won't tolerate this kind of behavior.

"We'll drive by their place to pick up your belongings. I've found you a new foster home. Let's hope, this time, you'll stay longer than a couple of weeks."

Yup, same old words. No one wants you.

Rule #12
Parents love with their told-you-so's

The newspaper rustles as he turns the page.

His wife plops the plate of hot food onto the table in front of him.

He raises the newspaper higher and turns the page again.

The wife spins around, pushes the swinging door open, and stomps into the kitchen.

Before the door swings twice, she comes back through. The light from the window glints off the instrument in her hand. She raises the object above her head. The scissors slide down the middle of the newspaper and stop when he looks up in surprise.

"*Híjole.*" Raúl Ortega jumps out of his chair with a news section in each hand. The late afternoon light shines through a prism that hangs in the bay window. Blues, then yellows, reflect on the badge on his chest.

Irma taps her foot on the hardwood floor as he folds the sliced sections of the newspaper and places it on the table.

Raúl reaches for her and wraps his arms around her, enjoying the feel of her wide hips and thickened waist. "I'm here. I'm here." He strokes her brown cheek and fingers the short curls that frame her face.

"Behind the newspaper," she says.

He cringes from the look his wife gives him, a look she saves for her delinquent children.

He lets go of her, picks up the newspaper, walks around the dining table, opens the bay window, and drops the paper outside.

"Happy?"

The prism swings in the breeze; sparkling rainbows of light flash across the wall. He kisses her on the forehead.

"Tell me the worry now, or feed your ulcer all night." She examines his eyes.

"Worry? About what?" Raúl studies his wife of twenty-three years, amused at how she reads him like a well-used street map.

"How old was the boy?" she asks, determined.

The youthful arrogance she had found so captivating in Raúl as a young man has been replaced with coarse, graying black hair, which gives him an aging-movie-star look. On days like today, his face shows his age.

"A girl. It was a girl this time. Jewel. Sixteen. She was short, not taller than this high." Raúl holds out his hand to chest height.

"And?" She pulls out a chair and sits down.

He shrugs. "Nothing."

Irma shakes her head. "No way you get off that easy."

Raúl folds himself into the chair next to his wife. "Shoplifting." He fingers the silverware next to the plate. "Had her hair all chopped off like she cut it herself. Wore enough makeup to paint several murals. Could barely see her green eyes."

He recognizes his wife's smile at the memory of similar remarks he had made when their two college-age daughters used eye makeup.

"What did she do?" she asks.

"Caught her running from the store. Remember Morales's place? The small fruit stand on the corner of 4th and Nopales?"

She nods.

The gates have opened in Ortega's mind, and the words race out, chasing each other. "We found out at the station she had money on her." Raúl pats her hand and sighs. "She had this funny look on her face. Like she didn't care what happened."

"You've seen that before."

His wife has sat like this and listened numerous times. Too many times. "Yes, but in this one, her eyes were more like looking into old eyes. She's seen more than her share already."

Irma considers him for a moment, then kisses his cheek. "The girl just went limp and didn't respond to anything. The kid expected the worst and was prepared for anything. Like one of those crawly things that curls up in a ball, and you can't get at it, no matter how hard you poke."

"The part that bothered you . . ."

"Why isn't Julián home? He's later than usual." Raúl looks around.

"He has a project after school."

"It better be a project, not detention." Raúl slaps the tabletop.

With concern in her voice, Irma asks, "Did you get a chance to talk with this girl?"

"The boy makes my hair go gray. I've had enough of his being in trouble. If he . . ."

The front door slams shut. A few seconds later, a hollered "Hello" follows with a thump from the sofa.

"Put your backpack on the stairway. Your stuff doesn't belong in the living room," Raúl yells as he enters the living room with Irma right behind him.

"I thought I could do some homework before supper." Their son catches the expression on his parents' faces. "What are you looking at me like that for?" He is almost as tall as his father. The boy runs his hand through coarse black hair and stops two steps up the staircase.

"Since when have you wanted to do homework any time? What are you hiding, Julián?"

"Why do I have to be hiding anything?" Julián's shoulders tense. He rolls them under his white T-shirt and unbuttoned striped shirt.

Raúl hates the baggy jeans his son wears. "Because I smell a rat." Raúl circles the recliner his children gave him a few Father's Days past and moves toward Julián.

"Must be from all those scumbags you hang out with."

Julián, looking down, uses the toe of his sneaker to make semicircles on the carpet.

Irma moves between father and son. Raúl stops.

Julián steps off the stairs and back into the living room. He snatches his bag by a strap and heads back for the stairs. "Why do I come home? Get nothing but grief."

"If you'd learn to act right, I wouldn't have to be on your case every minute." Raúl follows his son.

Julián stops in the foyer and glares at his father. "You just have to be on the clock all the time. Super cop!" He doesn't wait for the reaction that will come. He bounds up the stairs, two steps at a time.

A street scowl gathers on Raúl's face, as Irma grabs him by the arm. "Whoa there, cowboy."

Raúl jerks his arm away. "He can't talk to me like that."

"Talk like what?"

"You always take his side." Raúl stomps back into the dining room. He glowers at the plate of food on the table, and his stomach goes acrobatic.

"He's not a criminal."

Raúl thumbs his chest, still hurt by his son's remarks about his job. "I do a good job. I deserve respect."

Raúl turns his back to his wife and stares out the dining room window. The prism swings back and forth; spots of color sprinkle over his body.

The young cop who graduated with high hopes and big goals perceives life differently now. He had planned on being the one Chicano cop who would take youth violence in hand and turn everything around for his own people, for the whole community.

"My kid has it easy compared to what I see every day."

"Your kid is Chicano, too." She jerks away.

Raúl looks up with raised eyebrows at her sharp tone. "What a revelation that is!" He kneads his temples. "Irma, I just can't seem to talk to Julián any more. When he was little, it was easier. I'd be fixing the car; he'd hand me the tools. He'd come in and repeat every word I said to him."

"He has his own battles at school. The son of a cop has to prove himself every day."

Raúl sighs. "Everything was easier when he was little. I would put a Mickey Mouse Band-Aid on a cut; everything was fine. Now I can't even say a simple hello without it turning into World War III."

"Listen to what you do."

"What would you like me to say instead?"

His wife glares at him. "Don't give me your 'how to talk to civilians in distress' tone of voice." Her voice rises with each word.

He points a finger in her direction. "Don't yell."

Irma stretches her neck and stiffens her shoulders. "Why not? Because I'm a woman? Because I'm your wife?"

Raúl grins. "Because your mother would get mad at me if she heard you. It's enough she accuses me of ruining her only daughter."

Irma laughs past the anger. "You stinker." She reaches for him.

He puts his arms around her waist and smiles down at her.

She leans her head against his chest. "Big stinker."

"Is that your mother's assessment or yours?" He's still grinning.

"Your son loves you. He is really proud of you." She raises her head and flashes him her best smile.

"Funny way of showing it."

Irma strokes his cheek with the back of her hand. "He's figuring things out. You have to have faith in him. Believe in him."

"I don't want what happened to my brother to happen to my kid. My brother's life was ruined." He swings his hips.

"Ruined, no. Changed forever, yes." Her arms circle his neck, and she follows his steps.

"I want better for my kid." Raúl places his right hand at the small of her back and takes her hand with his left one and twirls her around the room.

Julián walks in, headed for the kitchen. "Oh, gross. You could at least close the blinds."

As Raúl tilts Irma for a dip, she smiles. "See? No romance."

Rule #13
All you need is self-esteem to make it in this world

Irma enters her son's room. "Thought you would like some cookies." She holds a tray out to him.

Julián grunts from behind his book.

Irma sighs and thinks, like father, like son. On her right is his dresser, cluttered with bottles of aftershave. She moves them aside and sets the tray down.

The wall is vibrant with color from a poster of A. Rod, a baseball star, another poster of César Camacho, a champion boxer, and a poster showing eggs frying in a pan, "Your Brain on Drugs," that he had to put up to make his dad happy. She's also seen the calendar of skimpily clad beauties he hides behind the door. On the calendar pages, Julián colored their blonde hair black and their blue eyes brown.

"How are things going?"

"Fine." Her son's head remains buried in his book.

"That good, huh?"

"Yup."

She watches him, his hair combed off his face, the thin braid at the nape of his neck passing the collar of his shirt. His bed is centered against the opposite wall, where he lays reading with his feet on the headboard.

She spies his backpack, the contents scattered across the hardwood floor. She counts three comic books in the pile and spots a class paper with an "A-" written across the top.

He crosses the room, picks up his backpack, and stuffs papers back into the bag. She counts the familiar moves duplicated from father to son. They are replicas of each other in the way they walk, hold their heads when they listen, even in the way they scrunch up their eyes when they're angry.

"What happened at school today?" Irma reaches for Julián across the chasm of a generation.

Dirty clothes sprawl in a path to the hamper. At least, he's getting closer, she thinks.

"We got a substitute teacher in English. She's gonna teach for the rest of the week."

Irma eyes the book her son picked up. "You're reading Sandra Cisneros' *The House on Mango Street* for your class?"

"Uh-huh."

One of the father's and the son's biggest obstacles, she realizes, is exactly how alike they are. Father and son compete in a world of violence, always fighting their way out of the verdict imposed on them by society.

"Did you get any papers today?"

He hands her the paper she had spotted earlier.

She glances at the essay on Julia Alvarez's *In the Time of the Butterflies*. "Very impressive."

"Dad won't think so." Julián flings himself back onto the bed. Papers, books, and pens hop in the air as he lands.

"Honey, your father works very hard for all of us."

"Dad acts like he's married to the job." He tosses a crumpled piece of paper at the wastebasket. The paper joins the dozen other crumpled nuggets on the floor.

"He worries about you."

"For me. Everything he does is for me. I know, I know. I owe him big time."

Irma cocks her head and appraises her son's mood. "Something going on?"

"Nope." He picks up his book and reads.

"Something at school?"

"Nope."

"Look, I had this conversation already with your father. Can we just cut the one-word answers?"

"Sure."

Irma sighs. Competing with his reading for school, listening to music, talking on the phone, and a body ricocheting with hormones, conversations with Julián are punishing. "I want to know."

"No, you don't. Not really."

"Worried I'll take your father's side?"

"You always take his side."

Irma laughs and sits down on the bed. She strokes her son's head.

"Mom, I'm too old for that." He pulls away from his mother's hand and smooths his hair.

"You're too old, but never so old you won't be my son."

"Huh?"

She shakes her head. "Tell me."

"What makes you think I've got something to say?" Julián opens another book and thumbs through the pages.

Irma arches her eyebrows up and down. "I'm a mother. Remember? I have special powers."

Julián grins. "You always said that when we were kids."

"You're not a kid anymore?" Irma pretends surprise.

"Mom, give me a break." Julián closes and tosses the book back on his bed.

"So what's with your father and you?"

"He really loves being a cop."

"Your father likes doing a good job. He takes pride in that."

Julián nods his head, keyed up. "But there are, like, other things than being a cop."

"Like?"

"Like, I don't know." He sinks back onto the bed. "Other things."

Irma rises and roams around the room, stepping over clothes, books, and a baseball glove. She restacks some books on his desk that also holds a computer, printer, and scanner. She wipes the dust off one of his trophies. Then she counts the different books he has read, notes the heaps of papers by his computer, and asks, "You really enjoy doing projects?"

"It's okay, I guess." He shrugs.

She grins. At least she's receiving more than one-word answers now. "How good?"

"Good enough." His shoulders work harder at shrugging than his mouth does at saying the words.

Irma grabs the inside of her patience and stifles her inclination to scream. She eyes the paper he's working on. "Tell me about this project." She points to his bed.

Julián glances at the mess on his bed. "It's a paper."

She squashes the urge to shake him. "Easy to write?"

"Took tons of research. I'm the only one who thought of doing it this way." Julián stops, takes the papers on his bed, and shuffles them into order.

Irma throws out another question. "Thought of what?"

"I went and talked to some people at the university. They gave me some material."

"Material?" Now her son has reduced her to one-word questions.

"Let me show you."

Julián jumps off the bed and goes to his desk. From the bottom drawer, he pulls out a large file folder of brochures, spreadsheets, and computer printouts, then fans them out on the bed.

"This one guy who's been studying the same thing I looked into talked to me for a long time. He called the application form something like a fund or a grant, something like that. I could get some money to do more research on my idea."

His excitement surprises Irma.

"Ronnie, Hector, and me, we went to the streets and talked to the homeless. That was the day Dad found out I wasn't at school." Brown eyes turn to stare at her with defiance. "We had to get this information. Anyway, we did this kind of survey and took what we got to this professor in the political science department at the university . . ."

Irma watches him, his arms waving, hands pointing, identical to her husband on the track of a good idea.

" . . . and he thought what we did was great." Julián sits down. "He wants to use us to do some more surveys for one of his research projects. This would help to get into college." He stops and looks down at the paperwork spread out in front of him.

"What's this have to do with your father?" She drags the subject back to home.

Julián flops onto the bed. "Dad wants me to be a cop. Cops don't read. They don't go for this kind of brainy stuff."

Irma laughs. "Who read to you every night when you were a baby? Who spends half of our money at the bookstore?"

Julián shrugs.

"Honey, your father graduated in the top five of his class at the academy."

"So? That's just police school. What's the big deal?" Julián picks up his paperwork and taps the pages into order.

"Your father believes education will change the world. Where do you get the idea he would be displeased with you furthering your education?"

"Mom, you just don't get the problem. I want to go to college." He looks away. "I might want to get into politics." At a look from his mother, he continues. "Dad doesn't like politicians." Julián slips the paperwork back into the folder and takes his time to match all the corners.

Irma chuckles. "Honey, *everyone* gripes about politicians."

"I didn't do any sports this year so I could improve my grades. That disappointed Dad." Julián's look is one of teenage catastrophe at its worst. "Mom, I don't want to be a cop. Dad's never going to forgive me."

"Honey, your father will be thrilled you're thinking of other things."

"Like he was thrilled today?"

She wonders how to explain something even she isn't happy with. "He was preoccupied. You have to talk to him."

Julián shakes his head slowly as he shuts the folder. "He doesn't have time."

She pushes a bit harder, hoping she doesn't lose him just yet. "Julián, it sounds like this stuff is really interesting."

Her son's face lights up. "Yeah, it is."

"Sounds like you're ready to go after what you need to make it happen."

"Yeah."

His mother drops the latch. "Your father's involvement is one more piece of what you have to do."

Julián's shoulders drop.

"You show your father how valuable this project is by how much thought you have put into it, he'll get the idea because . . ."

"I know. I know. My father loves me."

"That, too."

"He's gonna hate me forever."

Rule #14
A home can be any combination if it's filled with love

When Jewel first catches sight of the house, she suspects this placement might not be as bad. The house is big, two levels. Toys lie sprawled across a large front yard, and a station wagon sits parked in the double garage, just like the happy families in the movies. Maybe, just maybe, this won't be so bad.

The inside is as nice as the outside with a thick carpet in the living room. A big wooden table stands on one side of the kitchen so the whole family can eat together. Maybe, just maybe.

The foster mother, Mrs. Elkins, is tall and exercise-thin. She has just returned from the gym and wears leotards.

"We're so glad you could open up your home for Jewel." The social worker smiles and sits down at the kitchen table.

Mrs. Clarke pulls out forms for the foster mother to sign. This social worker acts confident, always saying the right thing, not like Jewel's mother, who's afraid of everyone.

"Well, I hope Jewel will be very happy in our home. We're looking forward to her joining us." The foster mother smiles at Jewel. "We're going to get along just fine, aren't we, Jewel?"

Jewel nods. She imagines her mother in their kitchen, cleaning everything twice, forgetting to get supper ready. But she tries so hard. She wants to do well so much; her intentions are good. No. Stop. Her mother can do other things much nicer than this.

The foster mother shows Jewel her room: twin beds, floral bedspreads match the curtains.

Foster mom points out there are no trees near the window. The closest thing to climb is a giant leap away.

Rules are easy she says. No drugs. No lying. No stealing. She glowers at Jewel on that one. No missing school. No boys in or out of the house. No being late. Jewel wonders if there are any yeses in Mrs. Elkins life.

Jewel's mother knows how to do yes a lot. Probably too much.

Mrs. Elkins hopes she'll be happy here. Jewel smiles.

Marie and Sara are the youngest foster kids living in her house. Norma, the oldest foster kid, babysits for Mrs. Elkins. All afternoon. Every afternoon because Mrs. Elkins volunteers at Legal Aid or something.

Everyone knows Mrs. Elkins has a big heart.

Rule #15
Whether you matter or not is up to others

Jewel watches how Marie and Sara dress for school. Jewel puts on her cleanest jeans and a white shirt, and even tucks the shirt into her jeans. She thinks she looks respectable, hoping to pass for ordinary.

Mrs. Elkins drives everyone to school in the station wagon and lets them out in front of the school. Just like in the movies.

It doesn't help.

All the ponytail girls wear dresses and whisper, "Another State Kid from the Elkins."

Punkers and skinheads stand off at the corner of the building. Smoking. Stupid lot.

A bunch of Chicanos and Blacks hang in their own groups by the curb.

Jewel stands between the people of color, the skinheads, and the ponytails.

Waiting.

One of the skinheads yells out, "Hey bitch, get your ass over here."

She belongs now.

Rule #16
Numbing outbeats pain any day

Grace Clarke sits at her desk in the rehabilitation offices. She runs her hand over the file folder and traces the letters that spell out "Jewel." This child is a thorn in her side.

The same words had been used to describe Grace. Her grandmother's voice, deep and mellow from singing gospel on Sunday mornings, still echoed in her head. Her grandmother would touch her cheek with that look of pride in her eyes. The one thing Grace worked hard to deserve.

"You're never going away, right?" Grace had asked her grandmother.

"Now child, why would I want to go away and leave before I see this lovely girl turn into a beautiful woman?"

Grace would snuggle her head against her grandmother's side and wrap her short arms around the stout waist. "I'm lovely?" She would breathe in the scent of her grandmother's perfumed talcum powder.

"The loveliest of the lovely. Just like your mother."

"Tell me about my mother."

"Again? You ever going to get tired of listening to your grandmother's stories?"

"No, ma'am. I'm never going to leave you. I'm going to grow up and make a lot of money to give you nice things. I'm going to get an apartment so that we can live together until I'm old. I'm going to take care of you forever."

"Whoohie, child. That's a big order."

"Yes, ma'am." Grace would nod into the soft body of her grandmother.

Her grandmother would stroke Grace's hair, flipping her braids through her fingers. "I tell you what . . ."

Grace would sit up tall to listen well.

"You grow up, get educated really good. Take that education and you help other little girls get educated. You give to them what I've given to you. What your parents have given to you." Her grandmother would trace her nose with her wrinkled finger.

"Yes, ma'am."

Grace slips the file into the holder marked "Current." If only she could get Jewel to stick with her until she's finished with her.

Grace sighs. Well, at least she's fine for the night. Tomorrow will be another day.

Wasted Childhood
by Jewel

A child
laughs and
runs and
plays all day.

A child
watches clouds go by,
jumps in muddy puddles,
walks between raindrops,
chases after butterflies.

A child
loves bright colors,
tells old jokes,
is smart beyond its years.

A child weaves daisies
into a crown to say,
"I Love You."

A child hangs macaroni
on a string for a necklace
to say, "You're beautiful."

A child sticks their hand
in cold plaster
to say, "I'm yours forever."

Childhoods are
sweet and innocent.
Full of loving hugs
and homemade cookies.

Childhoods are nice like
the fairy-tale stories say.

Childhoods can be taken
away so fast you'd think
you've never had one.

Childhoods can be nightmares.

Rule #17
Primary caregiver sometimes ain't your parent

Saturday morning and I am visiting my mom. State allows visits for two hours per week at a public place. The coffeeshop has only a few customers sitting at the tables. A couple reads the newspaper, trading sections as they finish one. My mom and I sat outside at the lower tables because Mom sways a bit when she talks.

"He was so cute. Such cute, tight buns. Small and hard like he was." She wags her little finger in the air.

I take a bite from my croissant.

"Hey, baby, when are you coming home?" Angela pouts. "I miss you so much."

"You started something big, Mom. You can't just make a wish and it's gone. Like your boyfriends."

Deep maroon polished nails wave in front of my face. "Details. Details. When you get home, we'll have a girl's night. Remember girl's night. Pizza and popcorn and scary movies. You and me, all night long." She giggles. "Never mattered if Jim or Henry or whoever didn't get the jokes. *We* did."

"Or Tom and Harry Dick."

My mom closes her eyes from giggling so hard and covers her mouth. She checks around the room but sees only women. "You remembered."

"Of course I did. You want me to remember for you. You always said that."

In the space of a second's tick, my mom's face melts into sad eyes and a drooping mouth. "You're my baby. You're the only one that understands."

"Mom, don't think about it. I'll keep the memories for you. Remember our deal: I keep the memories, and you don't overdose."

I look over my mother's shoulder and see one of the foster kids from the Elkins' place, standing in the doorway, beckoning me to come outside. "Hang in there, Mom. I'll be right back."

I step out of the coffeeshop, stop at the curb, and lean over to talk through the open passenger window of the Elkins' station wagon. "I gots to take her home. She's sick and I being the one making sure she getting home okay."

Alone at the curb, I pocket the bus fare while they drive away.

Back inside, I take my mother's arm. "C'mon, Mom. Let's get you home and in bed."

"But with who? That's the big question?" She laughs as they exit and turn down the street.

I hold her upright as we walk with our arms wrapped around each other's waist.

"Only you, baby. Only you have always been there to take care of me."

Rule #18
Stick with the State Kids, they know

The vacuum cleaner hums upstairs as the two other foster girls complete their chores late on Saturday morning. Jewel's chores are done because later in the afternoon she'll visit her mother.

Norma leans over to turn up the volume on the television. She sobs hard and takes a deep breath, sits back, blows a large, pink bubble, and pops it by sucking the gum back into her mouth. On the cable station, showing last week's soap operas, John Black and Roman are about to fight over the beautiful Marlena. Again. Norma hugs a cushion to her chest and buries her chin in the soft fabric. She takes huge gulps of air as she sobs and wipes at her eyes. Her mascara smears into raccoon eyes.

Jewel leans against the doorjamb, arms crossed. "You getting snots on the pillow. We in big time trouble."

"But . . ." Norma stops chewing her gum, hiccups between sobs, and cries.

They had cleaned the living room earlier. They ran the dust wiper along the ceiling and lights, making sure no spiders lived there or grime piled up. The vacuum sucked up every bit of dirt from the rug and the stuffed brocade furniture. They polished tables until they saw their faces in the shine. They took down the curtains on the two large windows, one on each wall, washed them, and put them back up.

The big family pulls together to make Mrs. Elkins' house appear homey.

Jewel studies the crying girl on the eggshell brocade sofa across the room. She has found out that Norma is seventeen and goes big time into the "normal" style. Once, Jewel leafed through the magazine from where Norma copies the style of hair and clothes so she can identify with the movie stars in happy families. Her navy twill trousers and light blue, long-sleeved button blouse is straight student dorky. She even has a matching blue headband that holds her blonde hair back in a flip style. The ends of her flip curl up to touch her cheek.

Unhinging slowly, Jewel crosses the room, and puts her hand on Norma's shoulder. "Things hard?" She has to act nice to the other kids in the house. If she appears to go along with the State's program, she's allowed to visit her mother.

Norma points to the show on the television, shakes her head, then nods, chewing gum the whole while.

"You clearing things up good." Jewel uses her hip and crowds Norma over on the sofa and flops down next to her. "How long you living in this house?"

"For over a year." Norma sniffles.

Jewel grabs a box of tissues. Norma pulls one out and blows her nose with an awfully loud honk.

When the commercial comes on, Norma puts her attention on Jewel. "How about you?"

Jewel yawns as Norma assesses Jewel's hair, painted in orange spots that match her sweatshirt and her cutoff shorts. Norma shakes her head when Jewel puts her bare feet on the sofa, which isn't allowed.

"I just get here."

"Silly. I mean before here. How long have you been in foster care?" She hiccups and grinds her jaw in a pulverizing motion. There's no hope for the gum.

"Hmm, in three other houses so far. Not find what please me."

"Wow! In how much time?" Her chewing speeds up.

"Walking out on my mom five months about now."

The chewing slows down. "Where's your dad?"

Jewel bites on the nail on her thumb. "He on a secret mission."

Norma fashions a you're-lying look on her face.

"For real. My father does millions of hours for the government. They send him places we not know because my father so top secret. Like he a secret weapon for the country. He gots a secret undercover name. Dirk Pitt."

They stare like bullies, aiming to find out how far the other will go. Norma breaks the competition.

Jewel asks, "Been in this system long time?"

"Shoot, yes. I got into the system when I was twelve. My mom claimed I was unmanageable." Norma pops the gum in her mouth at the same time she slams her fist into the floral cushion on her lap.

"Ah. This system gots many labels for the likes of us."

Norma peers at Jewel over the tissue she holds to her nose. "What does your record say about you?"

"Mom sick. Not able to deal with her baby girl."

"Stinks, doesn't it?" Norma leans her head against the back of the sofa, jaws chomping.

"What you doing that drops you into this fine foster care system?" Jewel props her head on her hand.

"I stayed out late a lot. My mom, she meant well, but she'd get to screaming and couldn't stop. Sometimes I think she's more scared of this whole world than I am.

"You consider we understanding things they not?"

"Might be. We have more stuff to deal with. I mean all they have to worry about is paying the bills and going to work. We have much more important things to think about all the time."

The bubble gum shows pink between her lips; she sucks the gum back in. Jewel feels bad for the gum.

"Yeah, like cleaning the house for Old Lady Elkins."

Norma nods like the oldest she is. "She's not as bad as some. At least, she gives us a good share of our allotment each month. Not like some of the others."

Jewel grins. "Keeps me in hair color." She pretends to rearrange the tufts of orange-colored hair sticking out of her head.

Norma doesn't hear her. "One time, I slept all day. Mrs. Elkins woke me up because she was scared. We had to have a heart-to-heart talk. The kind when the grown-ups get all serious, and they want you to share your deepest darkest secrets with them."

Jewel nods. "What going on?"

"Usual stuff. You ever think about how if someone has a broken arm or broken leg, that person has someone to carry their books or their lunch tray? They have people to help with the load. Then we have our injuries on the inside, where nobody can see them. It's hard for grown-ups to understand when we need help."

"Like getting recess from the world."

"Yeah." Norma examines her hands, open on her lap.

Jewel's unwilling to participate in her seriousness. "Where else you lived?"

Norma sits up, twists around to face her, and puts one leg under her, excitement showing on her face. "I was in this one place that was awesome. They let me make my own rules . . ."

"You joking, right?"

Norma shakes her head. "Nah, really. They figured if I had a hand in making the rules, I'd be more likely to stick by them."

"Did you or not?" Jewel stops slouching.

"For the most part I did. The foster parents were very good to me. They listened to me when I had ideas. They let me try things, you know."

Norma catches the bubble gum with her fingers, stretches it out, tilts her head back like a baby bird waiting for a meal and drops the wad of gum back into her mouth.

"Like which things?"

"Artist stuff. I'm going to be a great artist some day. You want to see my drawings?" Smack. Smack.

"Ah, not really." Jewel slouches back on the sofa.

"Most people don't understand them. I don't care, because one day when I'm out of the system, I'm going to go to art school and do really well. You just wait and see, I'm going to be rich and famous some day."

Jewel squints and appraises Norma to make sure it's not her mother she's listening to.

"Jewel?" Norma's eyes become quiet, and her jaws slow down.

Jewel cocks her head and waits for the question.

"Why do you talk like that?"

"Like which way?" Jewel draws her legs up and wraps her arms around her knees.

"Like with all that bad grammar. Don't you care how you appear to others? Isn't what people think of you important?"

"It to you?" Jewel sets her chin on her knees.

"Oh, yeah." The chewing motion increases.

"Tell why?"

"Because it's important to appear like I have my life all together."

Jewel chuckles. "Norma, we foster kids. We supposed to be messed up."

"That's when the self-esteem has to kick in. Those foster parents I told you about I was living with?"

Jewel nods.

"They used that word a lot. They told me I was a real survivor. I wasn't the type who would let anything keep me down." Norma's back goes straight.

Jewel slides back down on the sofa. "You believe such stuff?"

"Sure, I believe them. That was the first time anyone ever told me something nice. No one before them had ever mentioned how I take care to dress nice. After they told me all that good stuff, I took extra care to dress even nicer." Norma blows a bubble and sucks the gum back in with a breath.

"They broadcast those words only for keeping you in line."

Norma sits back and examines her. "You don't trust much, do you?"

"Never finding any one thing worth trusting."

"I've seen other foster kids like you. They pretend to be so tough, as if they liked being alone. They act like they have steel running through them, but usually, all they want is someone to stick by them."

"You picking me apart?"

"Nope. Just telling you what I've seen." Norma pops a quick bubble and chews.

"Good. Got enough grown-ups telling me what I think without you working my brain, too. Why you not in your self-esteem home now?"

"The foster mom got pregnant. This was their first baby, and the social worker thought I'd be too much trouble for her." She shrugs. "Do you ever think about belonging in a family?"

"Got a family."

"Don't you ever want to belong somewhere?"

"You do?" Norma's crazy if she thinks Jewel will answer her dumb question.

"I'm going to have a nice home some day."

Jewel glances around at the heavy wooden end tables and the coffee table covered with magazines.

Norma follows what she's looking at. "One of my own. With a nice husband who I can fix the house up for." Her jaws speed up.

Norma's singsong voice jolts Jewel, and she remembers her mother's dreams. "What about art school?" Jewel asks.

Norma nods. "Oh, yeah, I'll do that, too."

"You crying just now. What about?"

Norma points at the soap opera figures on the television screen. "All of that. It's so real!" She bursts out crying again.

Wasted Normal
by Jewel

I worry more
about those
who say
they're normal.

They act like they're normal.
They fix themselves to look normal.
They buy things to appear normal.

Then they point at every one else
that doesn't look like them
and call them crazy.

Rule #19
You can die from too much love

In the backyard, Norma and Jewel play with the two Elkins toddlers. Marie and Sara arrive home from school and go into the kitchen to get supper ready. Later, while Jewel and Norma bathe the girls, Norma tells her secret.

Norma has a crush on this really cute guy, and today, he asked for her name. So she believes—without a doubt—he's hot for her.

Marie and Sara come in when they're about finished reading to the little girls. "Norma, we're out of sugar."

Norma makes them swear they won't do anything else except watch the toddlers while she and Jewel run to the store. Norma is the only one who has permission to get the cash saved for emergencies from the top of the fridge.

Norma rattles on all the way to the store about the cute guy. There is going to be a dance at school and Norma wants to go with him. She imagines the whole scene: what she's going to wear, how cute he'll look in a tux, the flowers he'll pick for her corsage.

In the store, they go to the aisle with the lightbulbs because that's where the handsome boy sometimes works. They're each holding a box of lightbulbs when Norma pokes her elbow into Jewel's arm. "Here he comes."

Jewel watches him come down the aisle. He's sweet to the eyeballs, makes you have to swallow a lot.

He isn't smiling. "Excuse me, miss," he says. A dippy store clerk stands right behind him.

"My name's Norma." She flutters her eyelashes.

Jewel didn't think girls still did the eye thing, but there she is, fluttering so much she thinks Norma's going to fly off somewhere.

"Miss, one of you has to leave the store," the boy declares.

Norma is still in her dream world. Smacking on that stupid gum. Silly, dumb girl. She doesn't decipher the message on his face.

Jewel puts down the box of lightbulbs and moves closer to Norma's side. The heart side. There's going to be blood leaking from everywhere in a flutter.

"You live with the Elkins. You're one of her State Kids."

A pain in Jewel's gut grows bigger until it pushes so hard on her heart she thinks it's going to crush it.

"That's why you can't be in here together. Store policy, ma'am. It's easier to watch one of you than both of you."

Norma's mouth falls open like the tailgate of a pickup truck. All the sounds tumble out. None make any sense. Jewel hears the cracking as Norma's heart breaks and hits the floor. Jewel would hold the pieces together for her if she could.

Jewel takes hold of Norma's hand.

Dragging her alongside.

Dragging Norma away from the boy, the fairy-tale prince, who could have fixed her life.

Dragging what's left of Norma's heart behind them.

Jewel thinks hard for words to soothe. Words to take the sting out. None come. Her throat is as seared as her hope. You'd think fairy-tale princes would be kind. They'd know when a dreamy girl thinks she's in love with him and take a minute for gentleness. Not so.

At the grocery entrance, Jewel takes the lightbulbs from Norma's grip and lays the box on the counter. They walk out and head home.

Jewel waits a while. She offers, "He good looking."

Norma doesn't say anything, doesn't blink, seems like she doesn't even breathe. Halfway back to the house, she spits out her gum.

After a while, Jewel says, "He a jerk. No useful use for a wacko like him."

When they enter the kitchen, Sara asks about the sugar. Jewel fingers her mouth to shush her; then she pries the money from Norma's hand. Sara skips off to the grocery store.

Norma withdraws to their bedroom and sits at her desk. She opens her algebra book but doesn't turn a page. Her mouth doesn't move as her eyes view pictures only *she* sees in her head.

When Mrs. Elkins arrives home for supper, Norma plays "Go Fish" with the two little girls. She sits on the sofa and flips cards on the coffee table, not paying attention to the numbers. Norma never wins.

After supper, they put the kids to bed. Right after that, Norma and Jewel go to bed. The four State Kids are all in one bedroom. Jewel wakes up when Norma bumps her bed.

Jewel drags her eyes open enough to see Norma dressed in gray sweatpants and a baggy T-shirt. She walks to the window; it's dark outside. Norma sits with her legs hanging out and thinks a while, chewing her gum.

Jewel asks, "Why you sitting on the window?"

She wants to wipe the tears off Norma's face. The light from the moon makes her face white like kid's makeup for Halloween. Her eyes are dark; the bulbs burned out. Her lips are full like the ones boys talk about liking to kiss. All the boys except one.

Norma pinches the gum from her mouth with two fingers, then sticks the glob on the window frame.

"Foster mom get mad. A major dumb move."

Norma hints nothing back. She squats on the windowsill. "I bet I can reach the tree branch."

Jewel reaches out to take her arm.

Norma jumps. Empty air is all Jewel has to hold.

Norma lands with a thump and moans. She's hurt. Jewel moans, too. She didn't stop her. Didn't protect her. It's her job to keep all foolish girls safe.

The quivering erupts in her stomach, spreads to her arms, to her face. She's rattling inside of herself. Her legs fold underneath her, she's not able to stand. She forces her feet to go, grabs a blanket, and heads down the stairs and out the door. Marie and Sara follow her.

Jewel covers Norma to keep her warm. Norma will be all right. Jewel chants over her, "Evil spirits away with you. Only angels and good fairies visit my friend tonight." Again and again.

Mrs. Elkins pulls into the driveway from an evening of volunteering. Jewel's ears fill with the screams that come after the car door slams shut. After Mrs. Elkins takes over, Jewel goes back to her bed and lays with the blanket over her head, even when the police ask if she saw anything.

Everyone always tells them they're survivors. They're strong. All they need is self-esteem.

Everyone knows.

State Kids bounce.

Rule #20
Never let them know you cry

As she steers her car onto the interstate, Grace takes a swig from her travel mug and lets the hot coffee reenergize her body. No one answered when she called the Elkins home. Everyone must be at the hospital with the girl who jumped out of the window. The girl who is most certainly someone other than Jewel. The girl who will be all right.

Grace will not let it be Jewel. She spoke to the director of a private school, where Jewel will receive emotional as well as educational help. Jewel will thrive there. She will receive the kind of treatment that will foster her talents.

Please let the child be all right. Of course, the girl who fell is not Jewel. She can't be that depressed.

Grace takes a swipe at her eyes. The hot coffee makes her eyes tear. Jewel is going to be the exception in Grace's workload. She intends to turn that child's life around and make a difference.

Grace remembers, she sat at the top of the stairs of her childhood home when she was seven years old. Relatives scurried around on the floor below. The police discussed the search for her parents. Aunts and uncles had spoken in hushed tones since the phone rang, and the uncle who had picked up the receiver had listened for a long while. Some of the hush had the sound of prayer.

The phone rang once more. Somehow the sound of that ring had frosted the area around Grace's heart. She had known prior to anyone taking the call that her parents were dead. Wails accompanied the hanging up of that phone. Crying and shrieking from her mother's sisters and brothers. Men held big linen hand-kerchiefs to their faces while their shoulders quaked. Women clung to other women. Grandmother sat calm in her chair, rock-ing slowly. Their eyes had met; their hearts had known.

Grace wasn't alone. She had her grandmother. But five years later, she lost her also. Grace learned then what alone felt like, what it sounded like, how it hurt.

She was passed from relative to relative, whoever could man-age the upkeep. Or whoever needed someone to help with the housework. Or had an elderly person who needed special care. Or a brother, a son, a father, an uncle, one who needed to be hand-fed and cared for.

Grace had learned how having no one on her side meant always being wrong. Crumbs from the table. How having no one who really cared meant the frost on her heart turning to a solid block of ice.

No one to get close to. No one to mistake her for family. Stay-ing at a distance from everyone because there was no telling when they would leave. And they always left.

Grace will not allow herself to be cheated one more time. She won't lose someone else.

The hospital comes into view. At the parking lot, she snatch-es her ticket and rocks into a space. She runs across the lot toward the doors of the hospital.

Wasted Tears
by Jewel

I spot the social worker
inspecting me strange again.

What does the worker think she's here for?
For me?
For anyone?

She doesn't get
how bad,
bad can hurt.

She doesn't know
how lonely
alone can be.

The social worker repeats the familiar words.

Better pack up.
Better off someplace else.
Better I go now.

She sounds like
"better" is her middle name.

She never asks me if I want to stay.
And I do.

I declare I'm staying.
What I don't tell her is why.

To look after Norma.
To take care of her.

I messed up,
not catching Norma
before she jumped.

I have to stay and
make it up to the girl
who dreams of being normal.

Rule #21
Sometimes the truth is in what you don't see

Foster Mom: My goodness, I'm so nervous. An interview with an actual newspaper reporter. Do you think I'll come out on the front page?

Newspaper Interviewer: This article will be in Sunday's "Living" section.

FM: Are you going to take a picture? Should I comb my hair first?

NI: Uh, you look quite nice already. If we could start . . .

FM: Oh, of course. You career women are always on the run.

NI: Your name is Abigail Elkins, correct? You have been a foster mother for eight years?

FM: Has it been that long? Let me count. Yes, it has. My, time does fly.

NI: Can you tell us why you decided to become a foster mom?

FM: I saw a need and wanted to fill it. I wanted to share my good fortune with others. I knew there were children who weren't receiving the kind of mothering I had to give. So I offered.

NI: Did you have any training?

FM: Oh, of course. We attended the training offered by the agency. I felt other people got so much from the training.

NI: How many children have you had in your home?

FM: My husband and I have had sixteen foster children, and only one turned out bad.

NI: What happened with that foster child?

FM: The child had been on her own for a long time. We put so much effort into . . . Excuse me, it's still difficult for me to talk about her. We had such high hopes . . .

NI: What problems do these girls usually have?

FM: Drugs, of course. Most of them have a history of running away. Generally they're good girls; they just need a firm hand to rule them.

NI: Do the girls give you any trouble concerning sex?

FM: Most times, they're quite promiscuous. Some have a history of pregnancies or abortions. We have strict rules about sex in this home. Besides, I have my own children to think about.

NI: Do you have a set of rules for each of the girls when they move in?

FM: Oh, yes. We sit down and have a good talk about the way things go here. No lying. No stealing. No drugs.

NI: That works?

FM: My husband and I believe in good communication at all times. We talk a lot to each other in this home. We think keeping the lines of communication open is the best prevention.

NI: Prevention of what?

FM: Acting out. Most of these girls are in the situation they're in because no one paid any attention to them. A child has to feel she is wanted or else she will act out for the negative attention. Of course, any attention, negative or positive, is what they're after.

NI: Do you feel you have an impact on these children's lives?

FM: I should tell you that by the time they come here, they haven't been children for a while. And yes, I do believe my husband and I are good influences on them. It's a fact we've turned around the lives of several of these girls. They are crying out for guidance. We supply it with a firm but kind hand, and they appreciate it.

NI: Do many of these kids run away?

FM: Never. Generally, they run back to us after they've been with their families.

NI: Why do you think this happens?

FM: One thing most people do is underestimate teenagers. These teens comprehend what is good for them and where they can receive the kind of support and care they crave. They realize they have to pay dues wherever they are, but they are more than willing to do what they have to when they're treated with understanding and kindness.

NI: What kind of chores do they have around the house?

FM: Marie and Sara take care of the children. Norma maintains the house with help from the other two. And now that dear Jewel has joined our happy home, she'll assist Norma in the household chores.

NI: You can get teenagers to do the dishes?

FM: Oh, yes. It's very easy. It's do the dishes here or go back to where they came from. They know what is good for them.

NI: Have you every regretted becoming a foster parent?

FM: Never. It has been a spiritually satisfying experience for both myself and my husband. We're just thrilled when these girls reach their goals.

NI: How many foster children currently live in your home?

FM: We have four. Jewel joined us a while back. She's been a wonderful addition to our little family.

Rule #22
Being needy means you're human

"Jewel, wake up. Wake up. It's your mother on the phone."

Jewel rubs her eyes and, as she sits up, looks at the disapproval on Mrs. Elkins' face.

"Tell her she can't be calling here this late. That's inappropriate." Mrs. Elkins holds the cordless and points downstairs. "Talk on the kitchen phone. I don't want anyone else disturbed by this."

Jewel tiptoes downstairs, shuffles into the kitchen, and picks up the receiver from the wall phone.

"Baby, baby, you there?" Loud sobs wind out of the receiver. "Is that lady trying to keep me from my baby?"

"Mom, I'm here. Whatsamatter?" Jewel hears the click of the disconnect.

"I'm alone." Another sob breaks down into tears.

"What happened with what's-his-name?"

"Blay. Isn't that just the prettiest name?" A quieter sob fills in the space. "He promised to show me a good time tonight."

"You called to tell me you didn't have a good time. Mom, it's three in the morning. These people aren't used to phone calls at three in the morning."

"My own daughter is scolding me. I'm in a state of despair, and they're teaching my daughter to scold her mother when . . . I need you, baby. Can you come home?"

"Tell me what happened? Did he hit you? Are you okay?"

"Of course I'm not okay." Sob noises go up a notch. "He promised me a good time, but he never showed up. I've been waiting all night and nothing."

"Oh, he didn't show?"

"Go ahead, say it. I know it. You know it. I was stood up. I'm getting old, and he's probably with someone younger, prettier . . ."

"Mom. Mom. Listen to me, Mom. There's no one prettier than you. Remember your daddy always said there was no one prettier than you." Jewel raises her arm and shrugs to keep her robe from slipping off . She hears the click of a lighter and the intake of breath as a cigarette is lit.

"You're my memory?"

"Yeah, that's right. I remember the good parts for you."

"But what about the parts where he, he, did . . ."

"Those parts are my memories, too. But I keep those memories for you, so you don't ever have to remember anything but the good parts." Jewel leans her back against the cold wall. With the receiver between her ear and shoulder, she wraps her robe and ties the cord tight around her waist. "I do only the good memories for you."

"Tell me." A whoosh sound comes through the receiver as Angela sucks on her cigarette.

"Once upon a time, there was this beautiful princess, and her name was Angela. Her father, the king, loved her very much. He liked to stroke her hair and tell her she had beautiful hair."

"Yeah, when I was little, my hair was long, down to my waist, just like you had it. But then you cut it all off. . . ."

"Hush, mom. Let me tell the story." Jewel slides down the wall and sits on the cold floor tiles. "Only good things happened to Princess Angela . . ."

A half hour later, Mrs. Elkins stands at the top of the stairs, listening to the whispered phone conversation in the kitchen. She shakes her head and goes back to bed.

Rule #23
Not everybody's out to screw you, or are they?

Jewel stands to the side of the César Chávez High School entrance. Students shout at each other, scrambling out of the building like bees out of a hive. Drivers rev car motors, showing off, jetting out of the parking lot. She's been ordered to show up at her homeroom. When she walks into the classroom, she finds another student waiting.

"The paperwork is here somewhere," Mr. Tom Garner rearranges the piles of folders on top of his desk. "We can do the school forms later." He browses them, smiling. "A messy desk implies a creative mind."

She sits in a desk on the front row. "You making that up." She fights to keep her smile from showing.

The teacher's almost as weird as the boy sitting next to her. Tall and solid, the boy uses all his teeth to smile. She's not impressed. His hair is buzzed off around his ears, the top hanging in thick waves to his lobes. T-shirt and baggy jeans hide a body growing in awkward angles. She bets he trips over his feet. A lot.

Mr. Garner asks, "Jewel, has anyone ever told you you're a math whiz?"

"Yeah, dozens." She's on the alert. When teachers praise her, they want something.

Sizing her up, the teacher's eyes travel from her spray-painted purple, spiked hair to her equally purple tank top serving as background to her fuchsia lace shell. After his eyes return to hers from a journey down her green-and-white-striped tights snug in her black, no shoelace high tops, she smiles. She's not dressing to impress; he can peek all he wants.

Mr. Garner marches from behind his desk to lord over them. "So, this is the deal. Jewel, with your exceptional take on math, you could help Ronnie sharpen his skills. Oh, by the way, this is Ronnie Mendoza. He's a senior."

The boy shows teeth, smiling like a wannabe best pal. She puts her chin on her hand and fixes her eyes on the chalkboard.

"Sounds like a match made in heaven," Mr. Garner says and swings his hands wide to the sides.

She rolls her eyes and lays her head on the desktop. This tall thin man with his forehead gaining on his hairline grins. His tan trousers and crisp shirt with silk knotted tie add authority to his words.

"On the surface," Mr. Garner switches to a smile, "this may appear a bit out of the ordinary."

She raises her head. "Got a flair for the understatement."

Ronnie laughs.

Mr. Garner claps his hands, rubbing them like he found himself a treasure chest. "I have room 354 set up for you to use every day after school until the exam comes up in six weeks. I've obtained your mom's approval, Jewel. It's cool."

"My foster mother." Jewel frosts the words back to him.

Mr. Garner stops where he's pacing and snaps her a look.

"Can we go to the library if we want to?" Ronnie asks the teacher.

None of this has anything to do with her. She turns away and stares out the window.

"Yes. That would be fine as long as you're quiet." Mr. Garner steps in front of her desk and blocks her view. "You have a point you want to make?"

Wide-eyed, Jewel sticks a thumb to her chest and shakes her head.

Mr. Garner sits on his desk. "Good. You can go, Ronnie."

Ronnie pops from his seat, tipping over the desk, sets it upright, then trips as he turns to the door and catches his flying notebook on the way out of the room. The teacher and Jewel monitor Ronnie's hurricane exit.

Jewel gets to her feet. "Why I stay? I do all my papers deadline."

Mr. Garner grabs the desk Ronnie had used, turns it around, and sits down. He's eye-level with her. She's familiar with this technique, making contact at the lower person's level.

"I might add you've done an excellent job."

Jewel turns her student desk backwards and sits on the desktop with her feet on the seat, sitting a head higher than him. "My heart flowing with joy."

Mr. Garner ignores her words. "We should talk about getting you some grammar support, but this is about Ronnie."

"Oh, this the section where you talk the 'do it for the honor of the school' speech." She grips both her hands over her heart and turns her face away in a swoon. She's been watching Norma a lot.

"You know what amazes me the most about you?" Mr. Garner asks.

She acts uninterested. It's an art.

"You are as smart as your mouth."

Jewel glares at him with a nastier look than the lawyer boy received. "You working me?"

"You could make a big difference in Ronnie's life. He has a chance to go places. He's a prime candidate for the Hispanic Scholarship Fund, which will bring him opportunities he and his family never dreamed about."

She moves her jaws like she's chewing gum. "Maybe he not wear your dream very good."

"Like I said, smart flows out of you." He leans toward her.

She pulls back.

"I want you to understand how important this is for the boy."

She flips her high-top sneakers off, plopping her bare feet on the seat. "Me heart pounding for your words."

"Ronnie has the chance for something big."

"You say those words already." She's so bored—like any of this will change her life.

"When he was in grade school, no one paid much attention to him. So he slipped through most of his classes, but when it comes to writing, this kid is another Gabriel García Márquez."

"I not recognize a student named Márquez educated in Europe." Jewel shines her fingernails on her shirt.

Again the man lets Jewel's attitude slide off his back. She wonders whether he's part duck.

"He has to do well on the math part of the exam. This is where you come in. I would like you to work with him, give him a refresher course. Go all the way back and start from scratch until we're sure he knows how to do it all."

"Teaching him one plus one is three?"

The teacher nods.

"Me. Why?" Now they'll discuss the price for this arrangement.

Mr. Garner scrunches one eye tight and reflects on her, trying to read the fine print on her brain cells. "Tell you the honest truth . . ."

"Honest. Lemme see. Got nothing to do with what you're really thinking, right?" She bats her eyes; Norma has been teaching her best southern girl imitation.

The teacher pays her no mind. "Because he slipped through the cracks, and when people think of Ronnie, they think of . . ."

"Some slow-thinking, foot-dragging, word-slurring, backward, ghetto boy. Dark boy." Does this teacher think she has no eyes? That dumb boy is a total loss. When grown-ups speak to you like you're slow, the bad inside of you grows.

Mr. Garner chuckles. "In a nutshell." The teacher man slicks back the bare part of his scalp.

"He ain't?" There's no hope for the likes of this dumb boy. Not that she would share this with this teacher.

"Isn't. Let me show you this." Mr. Garner jumps from his seat. He rushes to his desk and hunts. "Here they are." He waves a sheet of paper over his shining bald top. "The forms I needed earlier. I knew I'd find them."

The lost forms are put on a mound of file folders. He flips through more papers. She's getting tired; he pulls out a single sheet.

"Read this while I go get the other form we need from the principal's office."

He's practically running through the door as she pulls the paper up to read. She doesn't really care; she's just curious. She slips on her sneakers as she reads.

The Other Side by Ronnie Mendoza

When I look from the
inside of my color,
I find faces.

Faces who judge me
who assume much about me
who condemn me.

When I feel from the
other side of myself,
I feel skin touch me.

Skin that isn't mine
Put on me by other people's
ideas of what I am.

I'm doomed by their thoughts
For they never take the time
to know me from the other side.

She swallows hard; this dumb boy has layers. She gets up to toss the page back on top of the teacher's mess. At the desk, she moves some other papers around and spots another poem sticking out. She grabs it and reads.

Reasons To Be by Tom Garner

Thoughts shared with students
peel away at the scab of unworthiness.
I expect their wings of freedom to come.

I open doors for others,
lead students to seek a better life
allowing them to fling against the sun.

Yet, my fluttering weakens,
my broken wings wrap tenderly
while others soar as I teach.

"So what do you think?" Mr. Garner asks when he comes back into the room.

She drops the sheet of paper. "I got a choice?"

"We all have choices in our lives."

"If we *get* choices," she strolls to the door, "like you grown-ups telling us kids so much . . ." She stops at the door. "Why not doing choices of your own?"

Mr. Garner does his squint again, snatches up the paper she dropped on his desk, and glances at the title. He looks back on her face. Pale.

"Seems if others got a door, the same door able to open for you."

Mr. Garner crumples the page in one hand and points his teaching finger at her with the other hand.

"Not need to lecture about touching other people's stuff." She pulls the door open. "Seem to me if you desire Ronnie flying high, you show him he not flying out there alone."

Wasted Actions
by Jewel

Teach numbers to a dumb boy.
Exercise in self-esteem?
Teachers never stop.

This may be allright with that dumb boy.
Maybe he doesn't mind being seen with me.
I'm not considered.
I'm not asked.

People assume State Kids are different.
If they treat us like we're bad or dumb,
why are they surprised to get the same back?

Simple.
No one cares to see,
we are invisible.

Rule #24
Real words come when all is quiet

Tom Garner is glad to arrive at his sanctuary, escaping both the bedlam at the high school and the traffic on Highway 409. His home is a two-bedroom apartment in a medium-sized condominium. Inside the kitchen, he sets down his briefcase, then opens it flat on the metal dinette table. He opens the cupboard and reaches for a bag of coffee. On the counter sits a coffeepot, a microwave, and a cup with one spoon. He pulls the coffeemaker to the middle of the counter and rinses the pot. As the pot fills with cold water, he looks through the window to check on his neighbors across the alleyway.

The elderly Korean couple next door tend to their backyard garden. In the next yard, a couple of kids play at war, staggering as if mortally wounded when one and then the other point deadly gun-shaped fingers at each other.

Tom twists his neck painfully to get a clearer view through the window to the yard past the one with the kids. The Chicana with beautiful legs, long black hair, and brown doe eyes is sprawled out on a lounge chair in her backyard, reading. She is always out on the patio at this hour, perfect timing for when he gets home each day from school.

He justifies his peeping as an important component to being a good writer. He needs grist for his mill. Everything is material.

With the coffee brewing, he goes into the living room. He snaps the television on, and Oprah's smiling face materializes on screen.

Tom slumps onto the scratchy-plaid, maple-leg sofa and props his feet on the coffee table. Oprah introduces a woman who wrote a book called, *The Psychological Motivation of Store Coupons and Why People Use Them*. She has several expert guests, plus housewives, who have developed complicated and intricate systems for finding, saving, and using grocery-store coupons.

"Oh, man." Tom clicks off the set.

He swings his feet onto the floor and stands between sofa and coffee table. His mind plunges back to another time.

Another time, standing between sofa and coffee table heaped with old, dog-eared magazines. A nasal voice requesting a doctor's presence in different parts of the hospital blared from the ceiling speakers. Another time, standing between sofa and coffee table littered with half-empty cups of coffee. A doctor with tired eyes, stubbled jaw, and looking much too young to be attending his wife, coming toward him with face full of sympathy and regret.

Tom had reveled in the big news when she announced being with child. He joined in the planning, pledged to be a different kind of father than his own, dreamed of hiking, playing, wrestling, talking.

The day after the first announcement, he had come home with a football, a baseball glove, and a Barbie doll with all the accessories. They had laughed over his excitement. He called it "their pregnancy." The beginning of the future "Garner Athletic Team."

Then the loss, the anguish, the total and complete sense of powerlessness as he watched his wife bleed the baby out between her legs. Time after time after time after time. Neither one knew whether it was his semen or her uterus conspiring against them.

The first time, they cried in each other's arms. The second, he held her while she cried night after night. The third, her girlfriends took turns to let her vent her pain. The last, they avoided each other's eyes. He stood in the middle of the hospital florist shop, hating the smell of all the blooms that surrounded him. A clerk tapped him on the shoulder. He threw money and a room number at her and left. His wife never commented on the flowers she received. Miscarriages, he had read, are very difficult for women.

There was no sense to make of any of it. A miscarriage either makes a couple stronger or drives a wedge between them that grows and grows until it splinters everything they have. She left him, and he didn't blame her. But then, who could you blame? At whom do you rant and rage when it's "beyond your control"?

He sways and gasps for air as he splashes through the barrier of his thoughts. Tom reaches for a coffee mug left overnight on the end table. He makes a face at the dregs at the bottom of it.

Back in the kitchen, he fills the mug with water and sets it in the sink to soak. He grabs a cup from the dish rack and pours himself some coffee. He picks one of his three spoons. After he stirs his coffee, he rinses his spoon and places it back in the dish rack with the one plate and the one bowl he owns.

As he sips, Tom listens to the sounds of the two young girls in the backyard playing at war. He reminds himself he must hang up something on the walls. A picture. A clock. Something. Even though he believes a kitchen only serves one purpose: fixing food and eating. When that's out of the way, it has no other use.

Memories flow over him. A warm yellow kitchen, smelling of baked bread, full of people and noise, comings and goings of numerous family members, of a grandmother sitting at the table, fingers splitting pods, peas spilling into a bowl. His mother, swiping back an escaped curl, stands at the stove, sending warnings, threats, and praise over her shoulder as each family member scrambles out the door early each morning. The sense of home settles warmly into his consciousness. Tom swats it away and spills coffee onto the cuff of his shirt. He yanks his shirt off and rinses the cuff under the faucet while he curses the foolish thoughts that distracted him.

He sits at the table in a T-shirt; the dress shirt hangs on the other chair, drying. He spreads out his students' papers covering the small tabletop. Tom glances at the names of the students and stacks the papers into piles. One stack is for the more-than-likely "A" students, but, generally, their essays are a boring regurgitation of everything he has said in class. Another stack is for the bewildered, but sometimes humorously misinformed. The last stack is for what he calls the unknown.

Those unknowns have the least resemblance to anything he taught in class but generally prove to be the most entertaining.

Tom reaches for the last stack. The first paper belongs to a student named Alfred. He smiles. He can picture himself on Oprah, pontificating on the importance of high school essays. He would enlighten her on how these essays reveal character and point out the indicators that prove beyond a doubt whether the student would reach adulthood with the potential to think. He would write a book, using these students' papers as the basis for his analysis. Tom would call his book, *The Mind's Potential on Paper: Word Dumping at Its Best.*

His stack of graded papers grows as he finishes reading each paper. The wording on one paper makes him sit up. He turns the page, reads some more, and a shiver plummets down his spine. It's the kind of shiver teachers hope to get but are surprised when they do. He checks the name and whistles.

"Why, you sly fox, you."

Tom turns to the last page of Jewel's paper and reads, "Everybody thinking something; no one talking to each other. Unexpressed words determining outcomes. How can love come back if words remain prisoners? Locked away from the ears of the beloved. Only poets can save the world."

He looks over his shoulder and checks the window for any faces that might be snooping. He moves out of the kitchen with paper in hand, down the hallway, passes his bedroom, enters his office, and flips on the light.

The blue, thick carpet hushes the noise. Two file cabinets are set in the corner, capped with stacks of files; a desk with a computer sits in the other corner.

Tom drops Jewel's paper onto his wooden desk. He sits on the rolling, padded chair and pulls out the keyboard drawer. Smoke-colored, plastic file holders contain clean paper, bills, and various writers' newsletters. A clamp-on lamp hangs like a watchful long-necked bird over the keyboard. On an antique wooden table, badly in need of a good scraping, set up against the wall between desk and file cabinets, are stacks of revised chapters of the future best seller that will make him an overnight success.

He turns on the computer and waits for all the start-up logos to finish. A mountain of paper conceals two metal folding chairs, which stand on each side of an open closet. An artfully designed combination of shelves are set into the closet with a compartment for toner refills, pencils, pens, various types of paper. Each cubby is empty. The supplies sit on the floor in a cardboard box waiting patiently for the moment when everything can be put away in order. Even labels for each cubicle are ready and waiting to be glued on.

He hits one key, two keys, then several in sequence, and waits. The floor has several piles of theme-linked poems and short stories, which will eventually be put in book shape to complement the future best seller on the table.

A poem he wrote a year ago materializes on the screen. He reads one stanza.

Words remain prisoners
Locked away from the ears of the beloved.
They are prevented from
bringing love back.

Tom sits back and reads his words, then rereads Jewel's. How could she have known? How could she have sensed his world about him? Was she a devil or an angel? She had written the same thing he had written several years earlier. Almost word for word.

A couple of hours and fifteen brown-clasp envelopes later, the printer spews out a list of labels to magazines and journals. Tom stacks the envelopes on the small bookshelf by the door.

Back at his desk, he takes a thin brown envelope, slips several sheets of paper inside, tapes the flap shut, peels off the last label and sticks it on the packet. He places the thin brown envelope on top of the others and goes back to his chair. He doesn't look at it or his resolve will disappear.

Tom saves his work on the computer, then turns the machine off. He steps in front of the bookshelf, runs his hand over his favorite books and tips out Denise Chávez's latest, then slips it back next to Manuel Ramos' book. In his bedroom, he finds his jacket. In the kitchen, under the sink he rummages for a large plastic bag to carry all the envelopes. Back in his office, he fills the bag with all the envelopes. He locks the door on his way out to the post office.

Wasted Quiet
by Jewel

Part I hate most about the quiet
is how the words come in the silence.
Words filled with doubt.

Clammy words touch my skin,
and the fears crawl with my goosebumps.

Words flood the space in my brain;
I drown in the rambling.

Vocabularies fill the room.
There's no air left to breathe.

I sit in the inside of myself. Alone.
Did I make these walls?
Were they gifted to me?

Am I here for the rest of my life?
How am I ever going to get out?
Should I?

Being alone in this world
makes me prey for all the wolves.
All the things that hurt.

Fighting with no recess and no time-outs.

I'm fighting every thing I meet.
Not able to tell between
the gentle ones and the killers.

Fighting is the only way I know
how to stay alive.

Rule #25
Loving someone is an open invitation to be hurt

Grace applies her makeup. She looks in the mirror and smiles at her husband sitting on their king-size bed. Her eyes wrinkle, and she messes up her eyeliner. Darn if he isn't still the best-looking man she's ever met. She's proud to be seen with him.

"Stay and have breakfast with me, baby girl," he suggests. "It's early. No one will hold it against you if you go in at the regular time."

She fixes her eyeliner and adds blush to her cheek. "I'll notice."

She appraises his black hair, clipped short, and how his dark eyebrows match his pencil-sized mustache. His teasing smile reflects the look in his brown eyes. God blessed her abundantly when He graced her with this man.

She passes the bed on the way to the kitchen. "Since you're up, have coffee with me."

Glen slips out of bed and follows her into the kitchen, tying the belt of his thick, maroon Turkish bathrobe. He catches her sticking a frozen bran muffin into the microwave. "Grace, if you didn't have me to cook for you, you'd die of malnutrition." He sucks in a lungful of coffee aroma and shakes his head in appreciation. "Mmmm, baby, oh baby. Coffee smells good." He grabs at her waist.

She pulls away, laughing at his playfulness. "Smelling strong is something you need to take care of, right off." She pats his hands away. This man has the promise of forever imprinted on his heart. If only she could believe in promises.

He gives her his crooked grin that holds assurance of good times to come. She pats her French twist, tucking in stray hairs. Once he said he loved the way her curls would come loose around her face by the time she got home in the evenings.

He was at Harvard, studying economics. She was at Wellesley earning her graduate degree. Acquaintances, who introduced them as a couple, liked to say they came from humble beginnings. She hadn't corrected them. It was just easier going along with their misconceptions.

She attended a campus party, and her date had been a real loser. She made her escape soon after arriving. Glen followed her when she left.

On the Boston sidewalks, people jostled their way in and out of the subway entrance. The air smelled of a mixture of car fumes and weather about to break out in storm. People, indifferent and occupied with their own problems, crammed the sidewalk.

She walked down the street, the wind dragging on her step.

From behind her, Glen called out, "Wait, I thought you might need some help." He held out his hand.

She didn't acknowledge his call; he might be the date's friend who wanted to talk her into going back to the party. She walked, leaning her body into the wind.

At the corner, he caught up with her and put his hand on her elbow.

She looked down at his hand as if she had been contaminated with a disease.

He jerked it away. "Sorry."

"Why are you following me?" She made sure her voice sounded colder than the wind that pushed at them.

"My name's Glen. I came to apologize for the bad time you had at our frat party."

Grace studied him with suspicion. "Why are you apologizing?" Leery. What kind of gimmick was this? She had enough of frat boys chalking up notches on their stick.

"When you came in . . ." He stumbled as someone walking by bumped against his back.

She squinted. This guy was some kind of nut. She had better be careful.

He sputtered, "Anyone as beautiful as you needs to be treated like a lady. Or royalty. I mean, it's obvious you're not the usual frat groupie . . . And when you left, I thought, maybe I would have a chance. . . ." He let out a breath. "Instead, I'm making an idiot of myself." He grinned with so much enthusiasm.

She took a step back and considered him. He certainly had a good line, and he seemed sincere.

The traffic light changed, and she stepped into the street. Better to just go on home. Much safer, especially if her date was any indication of the type of guys that lived in that house.

Glen followed. "I wouldn't treat you like he did."

She stopped in the middle of the street. Her face an open display of anger. "He told you about his offer?" She swallowed. She twirled around, searching in all four directions.

The light changed and horns honked; she didn't move. Cars inched forward. Glen grabbed her arm and shepherded her to the corner.

"He didn't say anything. I don't even know the guy. Just that he's stupid for letting the most beautiful woman at the party get away from him."

"Where am I? I'm not familiar with this part of town." She took a step, then changed her mind, turned, and went in the opposite direction. When she stepped back, she faltered.

Glen took her hand. "Which way are you going? The subway's over in this direction."

She looked up at him, misery and curiosity scrambled together in her mind. "Why should I go with you?" She glanced at all the people waiting at the corner, each huddled in their own loneliness.

Glen smiled, and the light changed to green. He talked nonstop.

"Your mom ever tell you about the bogeyman? One time my mom told my brothers and me a story and scared the bejeezus out of us. I wouldn't go out at night for a whole week. She could really tell a story."

"My mother died when I was seven."

The wind tugged at her coat and messed up her hair. This guy was persistent, but there was something different about him. Well, she could let him take her home. Just stay in public and dump him at the door.

Glen took her hand, hooked it on his arm, and walked toward the subway entrance. "There was this one time . . ."

Glen orders, "Sit down. Let me cook you a decent breakfast."

She stirs her coffee as she grins at the memory of the first time he took her home. He had spun yarn after yarn about his family.

She leans over the breakfast nook and kisses him on the cheek. "You take such good care of me."

"So eat with me."

Grace spreads jam on the muffin. "Can't. Have to get in early."

"Do you really think your supervisor notices you come in an hour early every day?"

"Probably not."

"You're darn right. More than likely, he probably thinks you can't do your work in the eight hours you have." Glen grabs her muffin and takes a bite.

She snatches the muffin back. "I don't care what he thinks of me."

"Woman, you care. It's why you go in so early."

Grace hates where this conversation is headed and, like most mornings, can't deflect it. "I finish a lot of paperwork during that quiet hour." She sips the last of her coffee as she rounds the breakfast nook.

Her husband grabs her by the shoulders, turns her around, and wraps his arms around her waist. "Social Rehabilitation is damn lucky to have such a fine person working for them. Your supervisor should give you time off."

They kiss; no words are needed for several moments.

Grace pulls away and scrunches her face. "You're going to mess my makeup."

Glen smiles. "Good thing you can always reapply the stuff." He grins and reaches for a cup in the cupboard. "Sometimes I think you work these long hours just to get away from me." He pours himself a cup of coffee.

"Right. So why, on most Saturday mornings, are you locked away in the den? A little work from the office you have to tidy up?" She rinses her cup under the faucet, looking at him over her shoulder. Let this topic die a fast death.

"I'm not as organized as you are." He smiles his heartbreaking smile, and she smiles back.

She always gives in when he smiles at her with that crooked grin. "You are one devious man, Glen Thomson."

"True. True. But as the Bible says . . ."

He waves his hand in the air. The coffee splashes over the edge of the coffee cup and burns his hand. He swings his hand up and down, then wipes it on a towel. He trails after her out of the room.

"Being a woman doesn't automatically mean you have to do more than everyone else to prove yourself."

At the dining room table, Grace flips through the files in her briefcase, checking her paperwork. "What world are you living in?" Keep him on this subject, and maybe he'll leave her alone on the other one.

She moves into the den.

Glen follows. "I have it hard as a man. You have twice as much to prove as a woman."

She searches through the paperwork on her desk. "Buying you all those books on feminism is paying off." Just keep him occupied, and maybe she'll get out the door before he brings up the conversation about their intimacy, or lack of it, as he often points out.

He chuckles as he sinks into the Queen Anne chair next to the fireplace. "I'm telling you I understand. It doesn't mean you have to buckle under to them. You have a life with me. Why don't we go away for the weekend? I have some free time coming. You're due some, too."

She holds up a folder and waves it. "Here it is." Good. Now she can slip out before this goes where she fears. She slips the folder into her briefcase.

"Who is it?"

"Jewel."

"What's she up to now?"

"Another placement."

"You can't save them all."

"There's something different about Jewel." Grace stops and stares over her husband's head. "Her situation is unique. Even though her mother hasn't died, emotionally she's been abandoned."

Glen snaps his fingers.

Grace pulls herself back from her reverie, looks at him, and smiles. She walks out of the den through the living room, sets her briefcase down, and opens the closet in the foyer.

"You're using Jewel and all your other cases as an excuse." Glen shakes his head and watches his wife pull on her London Fog trench coat.

She wraps her arms around his neck. "Have I told you recently how having you in my life makes the whole thing worthwhile? I couldn't do this day after day if I didn't have you to come home to." This is so true. This man will never fathom how much he means to her.

He wraps his arms around her waist. "At your service, ma'am."

"I've been warned about men like you."

"Have you now?" He pulls her closer to him.

"Mm-huh. Made me so curious I just had to marry you."

"Regretted it ever since."

"Mm-huh." They kiss. He holds her tight, and she curves herself to fit his body. "You can still curl my toes like you did the first time we met, fifteen years ago."

"Has it been that long?" He pulls back arm-length and grins.

She slaps him playfully on the shoulder, "Jerk," and reaches for her briefcase.

"All you have to do is call me. I'll develop a virus that only happens to black men, and I could meet you for a picnic. Anywhere you want."

"Don't tempt me."

"Woman, that's exactly what I'm doing."

"Honey, I have a full load today. I have to make sure Jewel gets settled in." She has to do her job. Work is her security.

At the front door of their condominium, looking back, she is filled with pride. After this many years, they still have so much. How many more years can it last?

She closes the door on his smiling face. Is she doing the right thing? She can't remember the last time they spent a morning lounging in bed. But the foster kids don't take lounging in bed into account. She has to go. She has a job to do. At work, she performs under a microscopic lens. She can't let anything keep her from honoring the promise she made to her grandmother.

Rule #26
When a teacher thinks they
know it all, students get screwed

Tom enters the teachers' lounge and nods to the history teacher, who sits to the side in an armchair, grading papers, and munching on a sandwich.

As Tom walks toward the refrigerator, he glimpses at Symmone Hughes, the health teacher, chatting with the coach on the sofa under the windows. His heart skips a beat. Tom thinks, I'm acting like a cliché now. Symonne looks vibrant and animated with a sunlight aura around her. The coach smiles, muscular, trim, with a full head of straight, blond hair.

Tom cringes when Symonne leans closer to the coach, listening. The smile on her face grows. She laughs when the coach leans back, seemingly satisfied with a tale well told. The story was probably about muscles, sports, and something else just as macho and dumb.

Tom fishes his lunch bag out of the refrigerator. He rounds the end of the table toward the sofa and spots the stack of mail that sits on the small table next to Symonne. The thin brown envelope sticks out between all the white envelopes.

Symonne looks up and smiles at Tom.

Every word learned, read, or seen by Tom evaporates from his mind. He nods back.

Tom takes an empty chair at the table. The science and the math teachers read students' papers. With these two, conversation ought to be imaginative.

The principal walks in and sits at the head of the table. Everyone quiets. "This impromptu meeting was called because there is some concern about the decision you made, Tom, about the Mendoza kid being tutored by a new student."

Tom unwraps his tuna fish sandwich. "At the meeting, you," he points to the math teacher, "agreed I could do this. I don't understand what the commotion is now. I know Ronnie from when he was in my homeroom last year."

The math teacher leans forward, her forearms on the table. "The new student's a State Kid. Unpredictable."

Tom pulls away from the math teacher. No poetry in numbers. Math is the only subject that kept him from the honor roll when he was in high school. "You told me yourself that Jewel is doing well in your class."

The science teacher slides a paper across the table. "Get a load of this."

The art teacher pulls himself over to see a big red A- scrawled across the top of the page.

Tom says, "See? This is what I mean. There's nothing wrong with the tutoring setup."

The math teacher snaps her briefcase shut. "Nothing wrong? This student should be a teacher's dream. But is she worth all the trouble?"

The art and math teachers push their chairs and lean back to gaze at the principal. He taps the table with a finger. "I learned aspects of her in confidence. I can't divulge student records."

"Well," the math teacher says, "We all work with her. We need to be prepared if she's going to freak out on us in class. That and this assignment puzzle me." She snaps the salad container lid shut. "When you mentioned the idea to me, I was willing to let you help out. I have enough students to manage. But after I learned who you picked to do the tutoring, I had to talk to the principal. We have much better students to do the job."

The art teacher and the science teacher look at each other with concern, then back at Tom. He notices Symonne leans forward so she can hear what is said at the table.

The principal holds up a hand. "I okayed this venture. After you and Tom spoke with me, I thought the tutoring would be good for both students. I don't see why you're questioning things now." The principal pins the math teacher with a gaze. "Didn't you tell me the last time I asked that she was doing exceptional work in your class?"

"Yes, but . . ."

"And didn't you," the principal points to the science teacher, "just showed us a paper by that same student that shows exceptional work? I don't see the problem." The principal leans back in his chair.

All of them look at Tom with suspicion.

"We have enough horror stories at this school. Everyone wants to be prepared. Do we have to name names?"

Tom sighs. "All right. Jewel has been a foster kid for about six months. Since last May."

"Everyone knows that." The coach looks around with a bemused look on his face.

Tom ignores the comment. "The school counselor spoke with me at the beginning of the semester and wanted me to find some project for Jewel. She's a bright kid, just wants to go home. There's nothing to her. Really." He looks from one face to another.

"Why did you ask her to tutor the Mendoza kid?"

"The same reason we have roundtable partners. To raise her self-esteem. I hoped she might come out from behind that tough shell of hers if I got her involved in someone else. She's also been hanging out with the skinheads, and I hoped that maybe Ronnie's group would take her in."

"Yeah, like that ever works," the science teacher blurted out.

The math teacher shakes her head. "What about the boy? What happens if she leads him down the wrong path?"

"Like most women," the coach says.

Nobody looks at the coach.

"I don't think that's going to happen. Ronnie has his feet on the ground."

"And his head's in the clouds. That's one reason why he can't handle math. The kid doesn't understand what is important for him to achieve," the math teacher says. Then, to the principal, she says, "Well, it's too late now. It's on Tom if Mendoza doesn't pass that exam. His parents need this scholarship to get him into college. Otherwise Ronnie is going to be one more statistic. A bright kid going nowhere."

"I'm backing up Tom's plan," the principal says, and to Tom, "Just keep an eye on them both. I want weekly reports."

Tom nods.

The teachers clean up from their lunch and leave.

Tom gazes at his sandwich, hunger a memory. He wanted to do something good for the girl.

A hand rests lightly on his shoulder. He looks up at the softest brown eyes he has ever melted into. His mouth falls open. She's so beautiful.

Symonne Hughes picks up a napkin from the table and dabs at the corner of Tom's mouth. "Tuna fish."

Tom gulps in embarrassment. Goodness, does he have tuna on his shirt? On his pants? He's afraid to look.

"I understand your concern for Jewel. I think you did a good thing in putting her with Ronnie. He and his friends will be a good influence on her. I'd like to suggest she be given the TAG evaluation."

"The Talented and Gifted group?" the coach asks in amazement.

Tom nods. He watches her pretty mouth moving, but he doesn't take in what she says. She looks heavenly this close up.

"Maybe we can compare notes and decide what to do about her?" Symonne smiles.

"Do? About her?" Tom blinks. Who is she talking about? He wants to talk to her about the two of them. If there ever could be a them.

The coach steps up behind the health teacher. The coach winks at Tom, then looks at her. "If we're going to show the movie on masturbation this afternoon, we'd better talk strategy. You wouldn't want me to give the boys any wrong information." He laughs.

She laughs.

Tom hopes that she is laughing at the coach and not with him.

The coach swings his arm up to place it around her shoulder.

She steps away, rearranging the batch of her mail from one arm to the other.

He changes direction, running his hand through his blond hair, not wanting to look foolish.

Symonne waves at Tom as she walks out the door, followed closely by the coach.

Tom shudders when he spots the thin brown envelope cradled in her arm along with the rest of her mail. He waves at the empty door. He slam-dunks his sandwich into the wastebasket. Darn! What seems to be able to flow from his fingertips dams up when it comes time to say the words. The rest of the human race is able to say what they want.

Why not him?

Why can't he express himself to the one person who counts?

Why can't he say the words that begin in his mind, rush through to his mouth, and push at his teeth?

He drops onto the chair, takes a pen from his shirt pocket, grabs his notebook, opens it, and glares at the blank page. He writes, words dashing down the page.

Wasted Fixing
by Jewel

Most people want to fix me.
Even when I don't ask to be fixed.

Some say
they'll be a success if
they make *me* successful.

They are intent on improving me.
Making me act proper.
Having me look sophisticated.

Their intent usually means:
They need me to fit into their box of what life is.
They want me to share in their lies.
The lies they use to continue with *their* lives.

If you think I need fixing,
please fix your own life first.

Rule #27
Learning is about more than your brain

Raúl Ortega hates waiting. The car's hot. He's exhausted and wants to relax at home with a book after a draining day at work.

After fifteen minutes of being exceptionally patient, he jumps from the car, and heads into the school building.

He checks each of the classrooms as he walks down the hallway. If the door is locked, he peers through the window opening. Down the hall, he spots two girls in dresses and short leather jackets entering the classroom on the left. He zeroes in on the voices that come out of the classroom the girls enter.

"I tell you I can't do it."

"You got to."

"I'm never gonna learn this."

Raúl Ortega watches from the door.

"*Mira, vato*, it's simple. Just look at it like this." Julián writes on the chalkboard, his hand dusted with chalk powder.

"*Híjole,* I not be getting that," says Ronnie, his son's friend since grade school.

The two girls giggle as they settle into desks behind Ronnie.

Julián shakes his head. "Don't pick up the *gabacha*'s bad habits, *vato*. You're supposed to learn how to do it right."

"Look and learn." A puny girl, who stands on the other side of the desk where Ronnie is, writes an equation on the board. "If you breaking all the steps apart, all you getting is adding and subtracting."

Ronnie nods. "Oh, yeah."

Raúl realizes that Julián is wearing the red Hawaiian shirt ablaze with yellow birds and blue flowers that he hates. The two girls, who entered before he did, watch Julián. They send messages to his son with coy looks. They flaunt dimples at him and heave young, plump-breasted sighs. Raúl wants to stop this ridiculous scenario. His son has to think of more important matters than silly high school girls.

In a university sweatshirt and baggy jeans, Ronnie leans forward on a desk pulled out of formation, set close to the chalkboard.

Julián and the girl stand on each side of Ronnie.

Raúl stares hard at the pygmy-sized girl in her red and white tube top, under an oversized man's white shirt, ripped-across-the-thigh jeans, and black laceless high tops. Her hair, combed to one side of her head, is spray-painted red. She has caked her face with pale makeup and garnished her eyes in black with green shadow. He moans at the sight of so much makeup.

The memory of the face comes back to him. She's the one he picked up for stealing at the convenience store. Jesus, Mary, and Joseph. His son is hanging out with a known criminal. What does that boy think he's doing? He'll ruin his future. The kid's so dumb he's risking everything and doesn't know it. Raúl has to try harder to get them back talking about things, or else his son might get in deeper than he can handle. Raúl has to stop this thing with that girl before it goes any further.

Raúl shakes his head like a bear being chased by angry bees. He walks into the classroom and says, "Julián, I've been waiting outside."

Julián looks at his father, then up at the clock on the wall above the chalkboard. "Oh, sorry, Dad. Had to work with Ronnie. He's getting ready for that exam."

"I've been waiting for a long time." Raúl stands at parade rest and calculates the algebra problems on the chalkboard. He prides himself on the speed it takes him. He remembers another chalkboard filled with similar math problems.

"Raúl, if you want to get an A, you'll have to do it faster than that," said the nun at St. Francis Elementary Catholic School.

"Pero nadie más lo puede hacer."

The nun moved on him like a locomotive, the ruler high above her head. "You are in America. Speak English. In this class, we won't have any heathen words spoken." The ruler crashed down on the back of his hands several times.

"Go." She pointed to the corner in the coat closet. "Make penance and ask God to forgive you."

Everyone in class avoided looking at him as he walked obediently toward the corner. His parents, speaking only Spanish, had preached that the nuns, acting for God, were always right. If he had trouble, he had asked for it. So for punishment, he knelt in the coat closet for speaking his own language and received an F for the day's assignments.

He finished his assignments faster than anybody else and was never punished again. He made the honor roll each year after that.

Julián exchanges looks with Ronnie, then walks toward his father. "Let me get my books, and we're out of here."

Raúl points to Jewel. "Don't I know you?"

Jewel hides her face behind a math book.

Raúl takes another step into the classroom. "You. I've met you."

Jewel looks up. "Me?" She points to herself. "I not think so. I choosy about who I hang with." She goes back to the math book.

Raúl's face sets in the resisting-arrest mode his son recognizes.

Julián says, "Dad, my stuff's out at my locker. Let's go," and pulls on his father's arm. They leave the room.

Raúl follows his son to his locker. "Why are you with that girl?"

Julián sighs. "I wasn't with her. I was helping Ronnie."

"She's bad trouble. She's headed nowhere fast."

Julián mumbles with his head in the locker.

Raúl pulls the locker door open. "What did you say?"

"Nothing." Julián swings the locker door shut, but the latch doesn't click. He turns toward the entrance.

Raúl puts his hand on his son's shoulder and turns him around to face him. "Don't turn away from me when I'm talking to you."

"We can talk in the car, Dad."

"We'll talk now. I don't want you seeing her."

Julián rolls his eyes and drops his shoulders. "I'm not seeing her, I told you. She's tutoring Ronnie for his exam. I was there because of Ronnie."

"That girl is nothing but trouble. I arrested her. She's a thief and a liar. She'll never amount to anything. You have a future ahead of you. She's nothing but a dead end. I want you to stay away from her."

"Dad, you're not listening. Again."

At that moment, their arms full of schoolbooks, Ronnie, Jewel, and the two girls walk around the father and son.

Ronnie says, "Catch you in class tomorrow."

Julián sags against the lockers. The locker door clangs shut. He looks at Jewel. She stares straight ahead. He watches their backs as the four move down the hall.

Raúl nudges his son. "Let's go, son. Your mother's waiting."

As the group nears the door, Jewel stops, turns around, and waits.

When Raúl and Julián catch up, she says, "Wanted you to get your son safest from my clutches. I liking my men older. So anytime you desiring a little more action, come find me. It fun being in the back seat of your squad car. With you. Again. You knowing where to find me."

Jewel curtsies, turns, and strolls through the double doors. Ronnie and the two girls gape at Mr. Ortega for a breath with their eyes wide open, then, a moment later, follow Jewel out. Julián stares at his dad with his mouth open.

"That little street hustler."

From behind them comes a voice. "Mr. Ortega, need I remind you that you are with impressionable children." The eighth-grade homeroom teacher stops beside them. "As an officer of the law, you have a responsibility to present yourself as a role model at all times. I would expect better from you, Mr. Ortega." She disappears through the doors, shaking her head, and muttering.

Julián hunches over and heads out the double doors so his father doesn't glimpse the smile on his face.

Wasted Sight
by Jewel

Ronnie asks if I feel bad at the cop-pop words.
I say no to that stupid boy. You don't ever
let it be known how deep the knife goes in.

People feel better about their own self when they have your
badness to analyze. They're able to avoid their own behavior.

Many lecture that self-esteem has to
come from inside. Which is thorny
to do when everyone is saying
the wrong side of true is me.

They climb on their soapbox and
preach what's good for me.
Yet no one takes the time to know me.
No one cares to find out.
No one stops long enough to
scope past the clothes,
past the words,
past the looks.

Their life is easier to moralize about me
than to take the time to find their own self.

Rule #28
Show your true colors
before asking others to show theirs

From the hallway, the rumble of conversations slows as students leave the building. The noise in the classroom is of a quieter kind. A couple of students sit in the back, heads close together, discussing a project.

"I asked you to stay because I want a report. How are things going with Ronnie?" Mr. Garner asks from behind his desk at the front of the room.

Jewel stands in front of the desk and flips through the pages of her notebook. "Fine."

"Just fine?"

"Absolutely very finest."

"Oh, much better." Mr. Garner grins.

Jewel covers her mouth as she yawns.

"I spoke with his math teacher. She's noticed progress already. You're doing a good job."

Jewel inspects her fingernails.

"Jewel, I'm here for you. If you want to talk or anything."

Jewel slouches over the desktop, stares at his eyes. "Oh, I thinking you someone maybe my mom knows."

"I would like to be your friend." He wants her to realize how sincere he is.

Jewel stands up. "You done?"

He comes around the desk and stands at the corner with his back to the door. "Jewel, you don't have to be alone in this world."

She tilts her head and looks up at him. "You coming on to me?"

Mr. Garner blinks like a camera capturing the scene. "No. No." He takes a step toward her, hands up, and thinks, then steps back again. "Your other teachers have talked about you."

"I in trouble?"

"No, nothing like that." The sound of words is what's hardest. He can think the thoughts. He can write the words. But saying them is a different route. "I mean your teachers are impressed with you."

"So?"

"I thought you'd be pleased."

"Can I goes now? Norma waiting for me. Mrs. Elkins asks us to be home fast after school." Jewel shifts from one foot to the other.

Mr. Garner thinks, is it her wall or his own he butts up against?

A smile spreads across Jewel's face.

Mr. Garner sighs, grateful that he's reaching her.

"Excuse me. Am I interrupting?" Symmone Hughes stands in the doorway. "I have a question for you."

Mr. Garner spins around, hitting a neat stack of file folders on the desk. The folders waterfall to the floor. Pages spill out of the folders, spreading the chaos all the way to Symonne's feet. His smile fizzles like a flat soda.

Ms. Hughes stoops to help pick up the files. Mr. Garner squats and scoops up the files around his feet.

She says, "I want to ask you about something I received in the mail. I thought since you're familiar with everybody's writing style, you might be able to shed some light on who the author might be."

He concentrates on picking up files. "Sure. Anytime you want me to read the papers, I can come over."

Symonne smiles. "I brought them with me." She hands him the pile of paper she picked up.

He drops what he had picked up, stands, and reaches for what she has in her hand.

She sets her briefcase on a student desk, pulls out a thin brown envelope, and hands the package over.

Tom lays the paperwork she handed him on the desk and reaches for the envelope.

He pulls the few sheets from the envelope and reads them quickly, spotting a typo. "Were they offensive?"

"Certainly not. They're quite beautifully written. But if the author is . . ." She looks at Jewel, then back at Mr. Garner. "You can understand the pickle I'm in. Can you help me?"

Mr. Garner senses someone beside him.

Jewel stands beside him, reading. She looks up and grins at Ms. Hughes. "Great poems, ain't they? Bet whoever written those must be liking you loads." Jewel nods her head enthusiastically. "Bet the writer of them poems would even like to . . ."

"You're excused, Jewel." Mr. Garner's voice is tinged with impatience.

"Who? Me?" Jewel smiles at Ms. Hughes.

"You can leave now." Mr. Garner looks at her. "Make like division and split." He steps over a few pages and takes Jewel's books off the student desk she had occupied. "Make like a ghost and disappear." He hands Jewel her books as she passes by. "Parting is such sweet sorrow." He points to the door. "Make me sorrowful and hit the road."

"Darn, don't he talk just like a poet. You think?" Jewel smiles sweetly as she walks by Ms. Hughes.

"Jewel, no comments are necessary." Mr. Garner feels his shirt wet at the armpits.

"You not think so?" She walks out the door giggling.

As the door shuts behind Jewel, Symonne turns her gaze back to Tom.

Wasted Fun
by Jewel

Grown-ups are funny.
They'll talk bunches about sharing
what's on your mind. Yet they're not able
to do the same.

What puzzles me is how grown-ups are great
with the lectures on how things get done right:
The golden rule.
The right attitude.
The path to success.

They have a whole suitcase full
of lines on how a person:
should act,
would act,
could act,
ought to act,
if only they . . .

Grown-ups never follow these rules.
They fall nose to the ground when
their chance to act comes along.

Rule #29
Depend on no one

Jewel jumps the two bottom steps and yells into the kitchen, "I'll be eating with my mom."

"Young lady, no yelling. Come in here and speak to us."

Jewel comes into the kitchen and spies Mrs. Elkins stirring the spaghetti. She waves to Norma, who sits at the dining table with her back to the wall and a leg on the chair. Norma made it out of the hospital with a broken leg, but otherwise physically allright. At the kitchen counter, she nabs a mushroom from those Sara is cutting and eats it.

Norma smirks. "Nice do." She points at Jewel's straightened, plastered-to-her-skull black hair with bangs down into her eyes.

Mrs. Elkins' asks, "How are you getting there?"

"I'm taking the bus." Jewel rocks on the balls of her feet. Sniffing hard at the strong scent of Italian spices, her stomach growls.

"If you weren't in such a hurry, Dad could take you."

"I not bothering Mr. Elkins. I gets there myself."

"Okay, go ahead and go. You have to be so independent, you can't take any help from anybody." Mrs. Elkins' shoulder muscles tense as she drains the spaghetti.

"It's no big thing." Jewel blows the bangs from her eyes.

"Fine. Go. Make sure you have the cell phone." Mrs. Elkins' back stiffens.

Jewel knocks on the chair Norma has her leg on. "How's life without the cast?" She steps out of the kitchen.

The wall phone rings above Norma's head. She doesn't reach for it.

Annoyed, Mrs. Elkins says, "Well, get the phone."

Norma looks over her shoulder. "Sara, get the phone."

Sara moves from the counter, swinging her arms as if great weights were attached to her hands and picks up the receiver. "Hello."

Everyone listens to a series of "Uh-ha's" and "Yups," then Sara hangs up. "That was Jewel's mother. She can't meet Jewel because some guy's taking her out."

"Hey, Jewel. You there?" Sarah screams.

More silence. Then Norma hears Jewel say, "Go to hell," and a door slams.

The three of them exchange looks. Norma breaks eye contact and traces the bleached outline of where her cast had been. Sara continues cutting mushrooms.

After a while, Jewel joins them in the kitchen.

"Oh, boy, my favorite." She walks to the cabinet and grabs a bunch of plates." "Have I ever telling you, Mrs. Elkins, that you cooks up the best spaghetti I've ever ate." She moves to the table and sets the plates down. "Except for my mom's, of course. My mom's the best cook ever."

Rule #30
Knowing the answer doesn't guarantee anything

On Friday, the school library is more deserted than usual. Jewel and Ronnie sit at a study table. All the other tables around them are empty. The librarian passes by, sniffs her usual dislike of Jewel. She smiles encouragingly at Ronnie, silently applauds his hard work, and leaves them alone.

"It's stuffy in here." Ronnie scratches his nose.

"Shut up and work the problems."

"It's too hard."

Jewel sits at the table and lays her head on her crossed arms, musing on Ronnie as he works at his problems. "Break it down into all the steps."

"This is stupid. They're not going to give me extra time during the exam to break down each problem."

"You does it in your mind." Jewel blinks. "Doesn't you want this?"

"Don't start on me."

"I means . . ."

"Don't give me any of that crummy talk. You have better grammar than I do by a long shot." Ronnie bends over the page and works on his problem.

Jewel taps the tabletop with the end of a pencil. The librarian appears out of nowhere and with a finger to her mouth, shushes her.

Ronnie scribbles on the scrap paper and writes his answer on the problem sheet. After studying together for two weeks, he has scored higher on a mock test than ever before.

Jewel crosses her arms on the tabletop and sets her chin on her arms. "Ronnie?"

"Yeah?"

"What you going to do with your life?"

"You mean *if* I have a life after this exam?" Ronnie erases the answer he just wrote.

"I meaning with the rest of your life. You thinking college or something else?"

He arches an eyebrow at her. "Just like that, you expect an answer." He leans his head on his arm on the table and mumbles.

Jewel nudges him with a pencil.

"I don't know." Ronnie shrugs. "Everybody's pulling at me to do one thing or the other. My dad wants me to be a lawyer. It's like no one's asked me what I want."

She spreads out her hands next to her face, palms out, thumbs under her chin, then smiles brightly. "You got to have an engraved invitation?"

He smiles at her. "You're different. You're easy to talk to."

Jewel kicks him under the table.

"Ouch." Ronnie rubs his leg. "You crazy or something?"

"You not making moves on me."

"Hey, I meant what I said. I've never had anyone listen as well as you do. I think you're awesome."

"I no kid. I can . . ."

"Yeah, yeah, you can hang in there with the toughest of the machos. So what? Big deal. That isn't what a guy wants in a friend."

Jewel studies him as he hunches over the page and reads the next problem. "What a guy wanting?"

Ronnie sits up. "Huh?"

"In a friend. A guy. What they hunting for?"

"Someone easy to be with. Someone like you. Where you don't have to put on any big front. You're easy to be with. I can say what I think without any worry about you holding it against me." Ronnie wags the pencil between his fingers. "You don't make me feel like I have to worry about how I am." He picks up the sheet of problems in front of him. "It's like these problems. They're hard, and I feel stupid every time I have to do them. With you, I never feel stupid. That's all. It's no big deal."

"It not?"

Ronnie grins. "In a way it is, and in a way it ain't. Isn't. But you know what I mean, you always know what I mean." He bends over the page and jots numbers.

Jewel reaches across the table with her hand open and stops just a hot breath away from touching his head. She traces in the air with her finger how his hair falls in curls around his ears. She can feel the heat from his body. She smells the mix of gym class, soap, and cologne. She wonders how it would feel if he did like her more than anyone else.

Ronnie looks up.

She points to the problem. "Showing you. Again."

He grins to his ears. "No one else but you can get this stuff through my thick brain."

"Your brain thinks an opposite way is all."

"You're the only one in the whole world who's been smart enough to figure me out." He pats her hand.

Jewel snatches it away.

Under the table, Jewel snaps the pencil in two. "Duh!"

Wasted Mirror
by Jewel

I frame myself in a mirror.
I don't comprehend what Ronnie discovers in me.
Why does he see something different
from what everyone else see?

Ronnie's goofy in a number of ways.
At heart he's the nicest, way deep inside his
soul where the real person lives.

Ronnie feels nice.
Ronnie feels scary.

Maybe, just maybe, there's a
place for Jewel after all.

Rule #31
Peace is never what you expect it to be

After classes end, Ronnie strolls to the conference room next to the principal's office. Julián walks alongside him. Jewel lags behind them. When Ronnie enters the room, he counts five other students who sit around the long rectangular table.

"What's with her?" A young man tilts his chair on its two back legs.

Ronnie hears him snort as he restrains from laughing at Jewel's spray-painted green hair combed back from her face, slicked against her head with Vaseline.

Ronnie smiles. At least her hair isn't sticking out in clumps like she usually wears it. He dumps his bag onto the table with a loud thud to distract everyone from scrutinizing Jewel. "This is my tutor. I'm supposed to be studying, and she's being cool about my coming here instead."

Julián pulls out a seat next to Ronnie. He twirls the chair around and plops down with his arms crossed over the back. "Everybody, Jewel."

Ronnie smirks as the two young women in the group appraise Jewel. She strolls across the room to the sofa on the far wall, acting like she doesn't know they're watching her. They make it obvious her fatigue pants with the knee-length sequin-sparkling sweater and her black high tops don't match up to their idea of style.

Jewel sits down, stretches her legs, and frowns back.

The young women gawk at the black globs around Jewel's eyes, then look at each other. They put their little fingers to the corner of their eyes to fix their makeup.

Ronnie looks at Jewel, then points with his chin at the boy in the tilting chair. "This is Hector." Ronnie goes down the line of people as Jewel exchanges stares with each one. "Oscar, Isidro, Raquel y Teresa."

Jewel yawns.

Teresa plops her arms on the table and leans forward, crushing the ruffles of her polka-dot dress. "This is a family meeting. She shouldn't be here."

Ronnie knew Teresa would be the first one to say something. He maintains eye contact with her when he asks, "Tell me why."

"It's obvious, ¿qué no?" Teresa moves her head to press her point; her straight, long, black hair ripples with the force of her movement.

"She's with me. That makes it all right." Ronnie smiles and spreads his hands apart.

Isidro, hair shaved on the sides and with a thick ponytail made from the strip of hair on top of his head, opens his notebook. He cocks his head to one side; the ponytail swings, brushing against his collar. "Are we going to have a meeting or what?"

"The first thing on the agenda is whether this newspaper is political or not," Oscar says.

Hector scrapes his chair back. "Of course it's political. What else does La Raza have but political issues?"

Ronnie speaks to Jewel. "La Raza means the race, our race, or us, the race we are. Like we're Latinos."

Jewel nods back at him. These friends of Ronnie have to think about what will happen wherever they go. All the time. No recess. No time off. They hammer out ideas, talking theories. They show how clever they are.

"We have other issues," Raquel says. Her blue-black hair curls to her shoulders.

Hector snorts. "Right. I forget. *Chavala* issues."

"Heavy duty girl issues, *vato*," Isidro says.

"Like they let us forget." Oscar chuckles.

Hector and Oscar slap palms in the air, laughing.

Teresa squints angry eyes at them.

Raquel slams a textbook shut.

Ronnie steps in. "This paper is for everyone and about everything." He takes control before the group turns the meeting into a party. "We are the voice for the La Raza Student Organization. We can make it look like anything we want. I believe it's in everyone's best interest if we invite articles from everyone."

The two young women nod. The guys wink at each other.

Julián taps the table in front of him with a pen. "I agree. We'll ask other groups to submit articles, too."

"Like who?" Hector asks, suspicion in his voice.

"I asked the Asian Student League to send some people to join us today to talk about it."

"*Mira, vato,*" Isidro says. "It's hard enough for us to have time together without having to share it with others."

"What 'others' are you talking about?" Julián stops tapping his pen. "'Others' like us? What we be told . . ." He stops and looks at Jewel.

Ronnie grins. Julián had just accused him of picking up his tutor's bad grammar. Now Julián fell over his own accusation.

Julián shakes his head. "What are we always being told about ourselves? How we're different from the superior race? How can we exclude anyone else or any other group without eventually excluding ourselves?"

"Yeah, yeah. He's right." Ronnie stands with one foot on the chair. "We have to stick together, or else we'll continue to fight among ourselves and get nowhere. If African-Americans stand up for us when we need their support, then we stand up for them when they need our help. It's the only way we're ever going to get any rights."

Hector pushes his pencil around the table with his finger. *"Mira, vato,* we hardly have enough funding for us, and to have someone else ride on our hard work could . . ."

"Make us stronger." Teresa glares at Hector. "You think the administration won't think twice if they encounter more than one color represented?"

"Think about it, guys. A union among colors is where it's at," Raquel says.

"All we're doing is asking for articles for the newspaper," Julián adds.

Raquel smiles at Julián.

Julián blushes.

Oscar catches the exchange. "But the articles they send have to contain something about *la raza."*

Raquel nods. *"Sí."*

"No way," Isidro interrupts. "How can someone else make a comment about us? They're different."

"It's real plain, *vato."* Ronnie stares back at everyone looking at him with a question. *"Híjole,* look at us. What do we have right in this room? We have *tres chicanos, un cubano, un puertor-riqueño, una mexicana y una chicana."*

"And one *gringa,"* Hector adds.

"We have to stick together among ourselves," Ronnie says.

Hector complains, "This is what I've been talking about, *vato."*

"Which doesn't prove much." Teresa smirks.

Ronnie stands. "We stick with each other and all our differences, because we're all the same inside. Where it counts." He taps his chest over his heart.

"We're all the same blood." Isidro thumps the air with his fist.

Julián stands up and moves alongside Ronnie. "We stick with other groups because we're all people of color. They're fighting the same battle we are. We have to fight whether we're doing it for ourselves or for each other. We help ourselves when we help those from another race. When one of us gets ahead, we all get ahead." Jewel understands that grown-ups put her into a box with all of their fancy labels. She never saw how it was the same thing they do to people of color.

A knock on the door halts all conversation.

Five students, who are Asian, walk in single file. Ronnie and Julián pull back chairs and invite them to sit. Teresa and Raquel pat the chairs next to them and motion to the two young women to sit by them. Hector turns to Isidro to complain and looks surprised that his *compañero* stands up and moves the chair for one of the young women.

"My name is Thanh. We appreciate your invitation very much. We hope you will come to our meeting next week."

Everyone stares at each other.

Ronnie smiles. "I'm there if my warden lets me." He jerks his head in Jewel's direction.

"If I can escape from my dad, I'll be there," Julián says.

Ronnie's hopes are dashed when his two friends, Oscar and Hector, avoid the newcomers by fidgeting with their pencils and notebooks. The two Latinas nod at the two Asian girls sitting next to them.

"Good," Thanh says. "I'd really like you to explain what 'La Raza' means."

"*Ándale*, now we're smoking," Hector says.

Wasted People
by Jewel

These friends of Ronnie have to think about
what will happen wherever they go.
All the time.
No recess.
No time off.

I hear them hammer out ideas, talking theories.
They show how clever they are.

All of them speaking of diverse ideas,
except they all want the same thing—to push the
walls holding them back so brothers and sisters coming
up behind them get an easier life when their turn comes.

Rule #32
Knowing how to learn is as important as learning

"Who telling you they think you not able to do this stuff?" Jewel asks.

"You need to read it in the paper? Cheez. We've studied these fractions for four weeks now."

"All I knowing is you not seeing the numbers in your head. You got to be figuring out a way to getting a picture of the numbers in your head."

"Easy for you. You make pictures in your head all the time."

"What gets you to speak those words?"

Jewel shifts her shoulders under her silver-studded black leather jacket, then tucks her fluorescent-blue undershirt into her tie-dyed jeans. Her legs stretch out in front of her, crossed at the ankles. The tongues of her high tops flap as she shuffles around.

"Because any fool with a brain can figure out when you're thinking you're using pictures in your head, if they just watch you."

Jewel leans over the desktop. "You the only fool smart enough to see."

Ronnie looks up from the math problems. He catches her grin. They sit in Room 354 at two student desks they have turned around to face each other.

"Still no big deal. I just listen to what you do."

Jewel watches Ronnie in his light-blue windbreaker and dark-brown corduroys, his body leaning over the page, erasing the marks he just penciled in. She shakes her head and stands up.

She moves next to him. He looks up at her when she sticks her open hand in the space between his face and the page.

"Why you acting like you not clear on what you want?"

"Probably for the same reason you speak so badly. So people leave me alone." He bends over and works on another problem.

Jewel stares at the curls on the top of his head. This dumb boy has more going on than she thought. She has to be careful with this one. He's sliding in where no one has been before.

"Appears like you going for the brass ring with college and all."

"Everyone seems to think I should."

She waits, but he doesn't say anymore. "No, never mind. Let me check how you done with them fractions."

Ronnie sits back as she checks his answers. "How many did I get right?"

"Pretty shameful. Got one right."

Ronnie slams the book shut. "Damn. Damn. Double damn. Why do I need this stuff anyway?" He stomps to the front of the room, then circles, trailing his hand along the wall. "They can take their test and shove it."

"Careful. A lady in the room."

Ronnie stops, looks up from watching his feet, and laughs as Jewel tosses her hair back like a movie star and makes believe she is sipping from a teacup with her little finger in the air.

"Excuse me, madam," he says.

When he's in front of the windows, he looks out over to the football field. "Football is what I'd rather be doing, but I couldn't play because of this exam."

"You good?"

He turns quickly and gapes at her. "Oh, yeah, you weren't here last year."

"I got no history anywhere."

"Last year, I did good. Real good. This is the last year I could have played."

Jewel sits on top of the student desk. "I got told you want to get to college. Like for writing."

"Yeah, writing. But that's the dig. You only hear about poor writers. There aren't many driving sporty cars and spending bills like they're free."

"For right now, playing ball is what you visual in your head?"

"Yup."

Jewel jumps off the desk. "I got a storm idea. Follow me." She snatches up her books and heads out of the classroom.

Ronnie grabs his books, stuffing papers into his notebook, and follows her through the school hallways. "Where're we going?"

She walks backward and crooks her finger at him. He rolls his eyes upward, stumbles over his feet, and juggles his books as they slip from his arms.

They squint as they walk into the sunlight. He follows her across the parking lot, and every few steps he asks her where they are going. She ignores him and walks past the fenced gate and up the bleachers.

"Who's them guys?"

Ronnie stands next to her on the bleachers and watches the players on the football field. "They're the freshmen practicing for second string. They're all aspiring to become great like me." He beams.

"Oh, puhleeeeeeze." She sits down and yanks at his windbreaker's sleeve until he sits next to her. "Now telling me what play it is."

Ronnie studies the field for a moment. "A tight end spread. They fake to the back, and he passes to the tight end, who's down the field." He points to a boy running down the field. "We call it the tight butt play. The girls like that, since they're all here just to check out our tight butts." He laughs, slapping his knee.

Jewel watches him, snorting his loud laugh. "You done?"

Ronnie nods, chuckling.

"How many guys on a team?"

"Eleven."

"How many running with the tight end?"

"Two guys to . . ."

"Block for him and run interference, I got it."

Ronnie eyeballs the puny girl with blue hair sitting next to him.

"One of my mother's boyfriends liked football a lot. He teaches me." She juts her chin out toward the field. "That leaves how many guys back on the defensive line?"

"Eight."

"Or?"

Ronnie concentrates on the field, then turns back to the girl. Confusion joins his usual doubtful expression.

"Eight-elevenths. Three-elevenths run up the field, and eight-elevenths stay back. When they all together, they eleven-elevenths. A whole. When they breaking off, they become fractions."

Ronnie squints down on the field, sits his chin on his palm. He turns back to Jewel without lifting his head off his hand. She shrugs and motions to the field. The players spring from their huddle.

The sun shines on the field; the boys line up for another play. Ronnie sits up when the play goes into motion. The linebackers move as one across the playing field behind the defensive line.

Ronnie points. "Those three guys are three-elevenths of the whole team."

"Yeah." She raises her hand in the air, and he slaps her a high five. "How you getting them back in with the others?" She sets her sights on him and holds her breath.

Ronnie scrunches his eyes, watching the boys get into a huddle. "You add up the two numbers."

The players take their position on the line.

"Which one? Top or bottom."

Another play is put into action. The halfback runs down the sideline signaling the quarterback.

Ronnie swings his focus back on Jewel.

The quarterback sidesteps a defensive lineman and pulls his arm back.

She sees he is getting the logic of fractions.

The quarterback spins the ball into the air.

"Top," Ronnie answers.

The halfback jumps into the air for the ball.

"Bottom numbers tells you the play."

The halfback catches the ball.

"The top numbers do the running around."

The halfback runs across the goal line for a touchdown.

Wasted Spine
by Jewel

I don't understand how no one gets it.
All that's needed is to listen.
People suspect if they show they care then
it adds more responsibilities to their lives.

Why is it difficult to say nice words to others?
How good you think.
How hard you work.
How much you are valued just for your existence.

Grown-ups are the ones who forget the most. Maybe it's
because at work no one tells them they do a good
job, they forget when they get home to say anything
good to the people they're living with.

Some grown-ups say they roughed up their kid on
purpose so the kid could face the real world.
Break the kid's spirit to make them stronger.
If the real world is so bad, why not just shoot the kid when
    it's born?

Spare the kids all the grief of thinking they are less to love.
Otherwise, it's like watching the kid die a little bit every day,
never able to make his parents proud.

Telling the kid they're worth a lot
is cheaper in the long distance.
Long run, sweeter.

If you fill the kid's spine and heart with enough love, there's nothing out in the world that can get the kid down.

That's the secret. If there's just one person in the world who's mindlessly, blindly, head-over-heels in love and enthusiastic about a kid, that kid is going to come out on top, no matter what they do in this world.

Rule #33
Romancing sometimes comes with two left feet

Tom rereads the note word by word. Comprehension escapes him on the second reading as much as it did on the first.

"Meet us after school in McCoy Hall. Bring your poetry."

Ronnie and Jewel had both signed the note. Beside her signature, Jewel had drawn a diamond shape with wiggly lines radiating outward.

Tom stops Jewel on her way out of the homeroom and asks her what the meeting was all about.

"Ronnie wants to show off what he learning. I telling him about your stuff. He share, you share."

Jewel walks down the hallway. "Going to be late for class. You wanting to get me detention."

He watches her walk away and shakes his head at her outfit. She has an orange bandanna wrapped around her head. She's also sporting a baggy, purple shirt with yellow ducks walking across in rows, and a floor-length, orange, tight skirt reaching the tips of her high tops. He's curious about Ronnie and Jewel's motives, since they have another week to go in their six-week stint. He decides to go along with their plan; it couldn't hurt any.

Inside McCoy Hall, Jewel, Julián, and Ronnie sit in the front row with their heads close together. The hall seats fifty people for small music recitals and school plays. They've dragged a chalkboard onto the stage and placed the large board so the view of the side entrance on the right is barred.

Mr. Garner steps inside; the three students stand up. Their beaming smiles belie the mischief he believes lurks in their behavior. With each step toward their huge grins, he feels increasingly like a lamb approaching a sharp butcher's knife.

Jewel motions for the teacher to sit next to them while she climbs up on stage.

"Gentlemen." She bows. "This afternoon, for your enjoyment, we have two special events. The first, an extraordinary demonstration of math brain power by our one and only Ronnie Mendoza." She claps, and they join in. "Followed by our esteemed homeroom teacher, Tom Garner, who's going to read his poetry." She pauses so they can clap again. Only Ronnie and Julián clap.

"This afternoon, the afternoon we have been anticipating, we will have the fair exchange of adventure, venture, and future. Let the games begin."

Jewel jumps off the stage as Ronnie hops on. He takes a deep bow. Jewel, Julián, and Mr. Garner clap loudly. Jewel whistles and shouts, "Bravo. Bravo."

"For my first act, I will do these problems. They appear to be totally complex, but with the skills I have chiseled out of my brains with the assistance of my esteemed tutor . . ." Ronnie bows to Jewel and applauds her.

Mr. Garner and Julián join in, cheering as if she had won homecoming queen.

Jewel slips down in her seat and hides her face with her hand.

"I will now proceed to solve these equations," Ronnie announces. "I might add, I have never seen these equations. I will answer them with the speed of . . ."

Julián yells, "Do the problems already."

"No one appreciates a true artist any more."

Ronnie steps over to the chalkboard, picks up a piece of chalk, and with a small bow to Jewel, he studies each math question. First, he fills in the answers for the algebra problems; then he draws the figures for the geometry questions.

Mr. Garner nods at each problem as he checks the answer sheet Jewel hands him. Julián and Jewel applaud again. From center stage, Ronnie bows from the waist, head to knee.

"Now, for the climax of this performance, I will flip the chalkboard over." He grunts as he flips the chalkboard.

Julián shouts, "Some feat."

Jewel shushes him with a poke in the ribs. Julián laughs.

"Now, I will proceed to answer this second set of extremely difficult questions. I've been informed, lady and gentlemen, that I've been getting these calculus questions wrong all semester. You are experiencing history in the making."

"Not if you talk us to death first," Julián shouts.

Jewel shoves him on the shoulder.

"It's okay. There is always one in the audience." Ronnie addresses to Jewel: "Us great math minds have learned to cope with juvenile behavior." He pushes the sleeves of his sweater up his arms. "Here I go." Ronnie puts chalk to board, stops, and steps back. "To make this even more exciting, my associate will time me. If you please." He nods to Julián.

Julián holds up a timer in his hand and shows it to the teacher. "It's set for five minutes."

Ronnie steps back and puts his weight on one leg. He reviews each calculus problem, then steps to the board and writes the answer with the appropriate mathematical theorem beside it.

Mr. Garner checks the answers on the sheet, then stands joining Jewel and Julián, who are on their feet, applauding and cheering. The timer beeps into the rejoicing.

Ronnie stands in the middle of the stage and bows, head to knees. He jumps off the stage and bows again in front of his audience.

"Good job." Mr. Garner pats Ronnie on the back.

Ronnie grins at him. "Now it's your turn."

"No, I don't think so. This is your moment to shine."

"Didn't you bring your stuff to read?"

Mr. Garner laughs. "Yeah, I've got 'stuff' to read. But . . ."

Jewel frowns at him, her head to one side and her arms crossed. "So it okay for Ronnie to take a risk, but not fine for you. It a double standard, no?"

"Is it important to you, Ronnie?" Mr. Garner asks.

"If you stick out your neck, I can stick out mine." Ronnie repeats the line Jewel coached him to say.

Mr. Garner swings his gaze on Jewel. "Nice catch twenty-two."

"Think it pretty good." She grins.

"Okay, I'll do it." Mr. Garner picks up the folder he had dropped on his seat.

Jewel and Julián clap. Ronnie bows and sweeps his arm in a gallant gesture as an invitation for the teacher to come on stage.

Mr. Garner climbs the stairs to the stage. At the center, he clears his throat and shifts through the pages in his folder. "What do you want me to read?"

"Any old thing," Ronnie yells out.

"Romantic stuff," Jewel says and kicks Ronnie on the shin.

Ronnie rubs his leg. "Yeah, romantic stuff."

Mr. Garner eyes his audience. "Romantic?"

"Yeah, we have to write some stuff for class, and you can be our inspiration."

Julián wins a smile of approval from Jewel.

"Okay, romantic it is." Mr. Garner pulls out a page and places it on top of the folder. He clears his throat and avoids looking at his audience.

Hearts True

Love is for the lucky.
Open your heart,
let my love flow into yours.
Let my love warm you for days to come,

allow me to cherish your dreams,
let me take pride in your thinking.

I rejoice in the beauty of you,
I shout with the joy of your being,
I clap with glee at the ecstasy of you.

You are my joy.
You are my existence.
You are love.

He gives a quick smile and slides the page back into the folder.
Ronnie, Julián, and Jewel applaud and cheer. They quiet
down as he places another page on top of the folder.

Beauty

Beauty for the observer
is the rich breath
of your sweetness.

Your loveliness
is the celebration of joy
filling the soul.

Your presence in my life
is the force that whips
my mind to a whirl.

Soul and heart yearning
is the anguish suffered by this fool.
The pain of words unspoken.

Too afraid to speak of my feelings,
I suffer in the abyss of words
shriveling inside me.

Were I to be princely enough,
were I to be brave,
words of love would shower you always.

"I'm done." He moves toward the stairs.

Jewel stands up. "No fairs. You got to be doing equal number of problems Ronnie done."

Mr. Garner looks over to the chalkboard. "Three more." He steps back to center stage and skims through the pages of his folder.

Jewel taps Ronnie on the shoulder. He stares at the teacher. Jewel yanks on his jacket, and he turns to look at her. She points behind the chalkboard. Ronnie pushes up on the arms of the seat to peer into the dimness. Julián nods. They spot movement.

Jewel points with a swing of her head at the exit. They crouch along the seats and move toward the door as the teacher recites his next poem.

Mr. Garner finishes his fourth poem and is surprised to see empty seats instead of students. He shades his eyes and searches for them in the dark auditorium.

"So it's been you all this time."

He turns and swallows hard.

Symonne Hughes walks toward him, holding a note in her hand.

Mr. Garner hunts again for the three students as Jewel shoves Ronnie and Julián out the door. Jewel signals an okay sign with her fingers, then tiptoes out.

"Maybe now you can read the poems to me in person," Ms. Hughes says as she moves close to Mr. Garner.

Wasted Sparks
by Jewel

Julián, Ronnie, and me with a bunch of
kissing arrows do the Cupid thing.
The rest happens like magic.

It's funny how grown-ups make loopy eyes at each other.
It would be nice to have someone want me with their loopy
    eyes.
Someone who would spark up when I walk into a room.
Mom says no other feeling in the world like
someone being happy you're around.

Grown-ups instruct on how first you have to find your
worth and pride inside of your own self, before you
can expect to find it in others.

Except we learn about self-worth by watching the sparks
in our parents' eyes. If parents have no spark
to give, we'll be searching a long time to find a
replacement to give us those sparks.

We watch others to learn how to give sparks.
Then we use what they do like a mirror to practice.
When they smile, we're happy.
When they love us, we're lovable.
Then we learn how to make the sparks happen for ourselves.
When we do well, we're proud of ourselves.
When we share, we feel loving.
Then, we receive sparks from both directions:
from inside of us and from those around us.

Everyone will be beaming and sparking.

Every day will be Fourth of July.

Rule #34
The northern winds
will always find the hole in your soul

"Hi, what gives?" Grace asks her husband on the phone. His voice is a salve to her weary soul.

"The computers are down. No one can do anything. So the boss wants us to go out in the field and reacquaint ourselves with the workings of the working class."

"Honey, what's the point?" Impatience infuses her words. She has to make herself sound nicer. Glen is being attentive.

"I thought you could meet me at the little Italian place for lunch, then take a stroll, go to the Alamo. Something."

"Honey . . ." I'm going to have to say no again, she thinks. How many times is this man going to tolerate no?

"Listen, before you say anything, I guess I sound like one of those guys that expects his woman to drop everything at his beck and call, but it's not like that."

"Oh, what's different?" Grace asks. A good defense is a good way out of a situation that can only lead to bad.

"This isn't about your job. What you do is important. I've always supported you."

"I don't . . ." Darn. Why did she have to fall for a smooth-talking man?

"You've always supported me with my schedule that's just as busy and hectic as yours. Bringing my work home. Being preoccupied. Granted. We both work hard. This is no attempt to discredit what you do or to ask you to disregard your work."

"Then what am I hearing?"

"I want us both to slow down. Take some time to get reacquainted with each other. Something's happening between us. Growing like a cancer. If we don't treat it now, it may get bigger than the both of us."

"Are you implying we're headed toward a separation?" Grace refuses to say the D word. She can't contemplate life without Glen.

"Not if it is up to me. Something's bothering you. I can feel it when I'm with you, but you're locking me out. I'm lost without you. All I get is your back on your way out the door. I'm worried about you; I'm worried about *us*. Are you listening to me? I want to be with you forever. To help with whatever is bothering you. We can deal with it together, baby. You and me, we're a team. Me and you against the world." He hums a few bars of their favorite song.

Grace smiles. "Glen Thomson, don't you be working me. I'm onto your wily ways." If she can only distract him, then the conversation will veer away from this thin ice one more time.

His humming stops. "This is no put-on. This is in earnest. I'm losing you; I can feel it. I don't have a clue how to stop it, and I'm busting my butt to get it across to you."

"Honey, I'd love to meet you. The agency just called about a runaway . . ." Work. The only solution to console her through any ordeal. Work. It never goes away. It never falters. It never asks more of her than she is willing to give.

"They don't have anyone else who can attend to it? You're the only one who can go?"

"Glen, I'm close by and . . ." If only he would understand, she loves him. She tells him. Often. Isn't that enough?

"Bullshit, you let those people push you around. They call you on every kid who gets in trouble; they expect you to jump right in. They make the mistakes and expect you to remedy the whole situation. . . ."

She stares out of the window.

After they first met, Glen had called a couple of days later. She had been surprised. And wary. He talked until he convinced her to go out with him. He approved when she wanted to bring her girlfriend along. The evening hadn't become too old, when she signaled her girlfriend to leave. That night was the first of many more. They studied together in the library on weekends, went to college games in a group, and tended to disappear before the game was over.

They had been dating for five months when he invited her to join him on spring break to visit his folks. She declined. He worked his magic on her, talking ceaselessly until she gave in.

The trip to North Carolina took a few hours by plane, Grace wringing her hands, Glen taking them and holding them firm.

Grandchildren filled the spacious house and raced in and out of doorways. Glen's mother, a small, thin woman, greeted them on the porch steps. Her curious eyes took in all that happened in her domain. Her ongoing banter spoke of Glen and his ways, all good: the straight-A report cards, the after-school job and giving his mother his paycheck, the first car he ever bought, which didn't run, the adventures of Glen and his brothers roaming the neighborhood looking for escapades in all the wrong places. His father was bigger than Glen. The older man had massive hands and broad shoulders, which bore the responsibility of raising five sons. From the pictures, she saw how his brothers had taken after their father in size. Glen was the runt at six feet, but the pride of his mother.

Grace felt she was under inspection during the entire visit. Questions came from aunts, cousins, and grandmother. How did you two meet? Where do your folks come from? You have plans for after college? How many children do you intend to have? The last question shocked her. Everyone at the dinner table laughed at the expression on her face.

Mr. Thomson asked his son to help him haul a piece of machinery from a neighbor's yard. Grace was caught alone with Glen's mother on the back porch.

"I see all my dreams in him." Mrs. Thomson stood straight and stared out across the yard at her two men. "He's the only one who's gone on to college. All of his brothers contribute to the tuition when they can. This family's mighty proud of him."

She spun around and eyed Grace. "Glen tells me you have no family."

Grace puffed herself up. "No ma'am, I have plenty of family."

"Who raised you?"

"My grandmother. Then when she died, my aunts did. My folks died when I was seven. My grandmother took care of me after that. I traveled with her and saw quite a bit of the world." Grace rubbed her eyes at the mention of her grandmother. "She introduced me to the classics, and I read my 'First Readers' to her. We would listen to music at night. She would tell me all the talents of each composer."

The sun moved behind a gathering of clouds. The porch fell into shadow. The shadows kept Grace from studying Mrs. Thomson's face. When Grace heard her voice, she was startled.

"Sit down, tell me about it," Mrs. Thomson said.

Grace took the chair; Mrs. Thomson sat in a rocking chair next to her. "Nothing to say, really." Grace smiled to take the sting out of her words.

"Honey, there's always something to tell."

Grace sighed. "While other kids played all summer, my grandmother and I traveled to Europe and visited museums, attended concerts, ballets. I had opportunities others only dreamed about."

"Hard to come back to school?"

Grace didn't answer. Mrs. Thomson seemed to intuit the truth somehow.

"How long were you with your grandmother?"

"She died when I was twelve. I worked during summers after that, so I worked the loss away."

Mrs. Thomson rocked steadily. "Loss is hard no matter what."

"I knew she was ill, so her death wasn't a big surprise to me."

Mrs. Thomson picked up her knitting. "Loss, expected or not, hurts. You get so you're used to not counting on anything. These Thomsons have a reputation for living a long time. They're the kind who hang on forever. They tell you they're going to stick around; you can count on it.

"My Amos courted me for three years. I thought anyone with that much perseverance was worth the risk. He's firm about his beliefs, but he's a good listener. I never knew how good that could be. Makes all the difference in the world." She turned her face toward Grace. "My Glen's just like his father. Determines what he wants and goes after it. When he sets his mind, there's no telling him otherwise." She rocked in the chair; the knitting needles moved so fast they clacked like a conversation. "I'm an honest woman who's been speaking her own mind for so long, there's no use in trying to act different."

Grace gripped the arms of her chair.

"Glen says he's in love with you."

"He hasn't said a word to me."

Mrs. Thomson waved her comment away. "Glen's so full of you, he can't see the pain in your history."

Grace stiffened.

"He'll do good for you. Just as long as you are honest with yourself first, you'll do well for him. Now that I've met you, I won't worry. Glen will give you a decent life. You'll never have to fret about that."

"I also have a career."

"That's between the two of you. I'm talking about what's going on inside of you. My Glen trusts you. He believes his love can cast out whatever is bothering you."

"He's told you this?"

Mrs. Thomson smiled. "Glen only talks about how wonderful you are. But I can see your pain, and I know my son."

The afternoon heat shot down from the sun and ricocheted up from the ground. The sounds and words from the neighbor's yard filled the space between Grace and Glen's mother.

"I come from the same pain. My parents died when I was four. Got handed around from relative to relative. Never felt like I was wanted anywhere. Got used by whoever was biggest. Always had to hide how I felt. Always felt alone. Never had a chance to really get close to anyone. Never had a chance to get to know myself. Until Amos."

A cat ran across the yard, stopped, dropped to the ground, and stalked his prey, invisible in the grass.

"Amos taught me about being around for each other. Glen can do the same for you. If you let him."

"You make it sound like I'm getting all the good in this relationship."

The sun snapped out from behind the clouds as the two men walked across the yard. The cat shot between their boots, which caused Glen to trip.

Mrs. Thomson's laugh carried across the yard. "Girl, of course I do. He's my son."

Glen grinned as they laughed at him.

A few months after the visit, Glen proposed. He never knew the reason Grace asked him to wait a day for her answer. She felt the need to speak with his mother first.

His mother had warned her that Glen would want all of her. Grace believed this type of relationship was what she had been waiting for all her life: someone that wanted her inside and out, soul and mind.

Five years later, Grace was Glen's rock when his mother died.

A cloud floats by and shadows the tree. The sound of Glen's words travel across her memories, "I'm fed up with this conversation. The same words going around in a circle, like the nowhere we're going. I want something definite from you."

"Honey, we can talk tonight." Postpone. Maybe he'll forget.

"No, you'll claim you're too tired from all the running around you do. I'm going to wait for you at the restaurant. If you're there, great. If you're not . . ."

The door shuts on her memories. "If not, what?" An ultimatum? Her back stiffens with arrogance. She doesn't take to ultimatums. She'll spit back in his face, in spite of the loss she fears.

"I don't know. But we can't go on like this. I miss you. I want you in my life, but not on a temporary basis. We're in this together, or we're not. It's your decision."

"Glen, I can meet you tomorrow. Today is just too hectic." He'll be more sensible tomorrow. Maybe he'll have forgotten the argument by then.

"I'll be waiting."

The phone clicks in her ear.

Wasted Solitude
by Jewel

Alone in the inside.
Alone on the outside.
Doesn't make a difference on which side I feel alone.
Lonely hurts awful on either side.

When the loneliness is in and outside of me,
it feels harsh.
How much alone does a person have to feel before wanting
   to end it all?
Must be some kind of cargo to carry.
Must be a load of no hope in the heart.

Anyone can do alone for part of the day.
But alone with no one to care if you're alive or not,
alone without family to listen with heart,
that's the hardest.

Rule #35
Beauty is as deep as your checkbook

Joylene

I just stood and couldn't believe my eyes. On her first day at school and she, like, just walked right over to those totally gross skinheads and started talking with them. As if it didn't matter how utterly important it was who you were seen with. I mean, like really, she didn't even consider the possibility of what it meant to be seen talking with them. I mean, a complete total dunce can figure that out. Like, how can you expect anything from someone looking crazy and weird?

What're we supposed to do? Like, you didn't expect us to put our reps on the line for a total unknown, did you?

Stephanie

We knew she was coming. Everybody at school knew she was coming. Every time the Elkins get a new foster kid, everybody knows. It wasn't like we weren't expecting her. She had to know that. We had heard about her. We knew about all the men. We knew about the drugs. Everyone knew. We told them.

Come on. She's a State Kid. She had to have drugs. We're not dunces, you know. We heard about their having babies all the time. They just drop 'em at the hospital. If not in some back alley. Everyone knows that. We thought she might be different. We kept an open mind. Even knowing all that. Every time it's the same.

166

State Kids are all the same. Everyone knew we were right. We told them.

Desiree

Lord, I was not going to talk with her. Did you see what she was wearing? God, I would not be caught dead in an outfit like that. Not to mention her hair. Mother Lord, did you ever see such a terrific mess of hair? You don't think she did that herself?

God, you'd think they never take her to a beauty shop or nothing. Lord, how can she even live looking so bad? I would just about die with humiliation. I'd never come out. Nothing and nobody could make me come out in public like that. God Almighty, a person has to have some pride in her appearance, or what else is there? Lord, no telling where she's been. Or worst yet, who she's been with. God knows what diseases she might be carrying. She is a State Kid. Christ, you just never know with them.

Tiffany

All of you are welcome to do what you want. But I intend to ignore her. If she's smart, she will know. Everyone admires us. All of you know what I'm talking about. Who else is there to hang with but us? Nobody. Just nobody.

All of you are just so obvious. Gawking at her as if she mattered. Don't pay her any attention. Someone will think we want her to join us. That would be a fate worse than no date on prom night. All of you know it's true. Those people have to remember where they belong.

All of you have to draw the line at some point. Before you know it, they will infiltrate everything. Then, where would we live? It is bad enough we have to let them in the same school with us. State Kids are in a class of their own.

Joylene

It's been a couple of months since she arrived. You'd think the State Kid would get the picture. The whole scene was so totally gross. Like really, it just never occurred to anyone to check. Who would have thought! Like, I mean, if you were just sitting there, wouldn't you have coughed or something? Like it was the ultimate in embarrassment. It wasn't like we meant to do any harm. Talking, we were just talking. That's all. It was the max in gross behavior. I mean, you just know, anyone else would have just walked right on out. But no, you can count on a State Kid making a bad situation worse. She just couldn't leave it alone. What were we supposed to do? You didn't expect us to apologize or anything?

Stephanie

We didn't know. None of us did. Else we wouldn't have done it. We're not dunces. Everyone knows we're innocent. We're not the type. Who ever! Everyone knows how it was. Poor Tiffany.

Those State Kids will do anything. She's proven that now. We were willing to forget her past. Everyone knows about her past. We told them. We were willing to be nice to her. We were going to do that for her. Did she appreciate it? No, she did not.

Everyone said she would be like the other State Kids. We didn't know what to do. Just like so. Out of the blue. Who would have known? Everyone suspected it. We were naïve. We were hopeful. Just goes to prove. Everyone said it. Some you just can't help. We knew. Everyone knew. We told them the *real* story.

Desiree

Lord, save my soul, I was not going to deal with that kind of behavior. God Almighty, did you see what she had on? Lord, what a mess she was. Poor Tiffany, too.

I wouldn't be caught dead looking, like, all scruffy, like they were when it was all over. Not to mention the proper way to act. We were combing our hair—something she could take lessons in—

and she pops out. Joylene's so nervous, she giggles. Stephanie shrieking the whole while. Lord, you'd think we were killing someone.

There was no almighty reason to get so upset about that. We were just talking. Among ourselves. It's our God-given American right. But how would she know? She's a State Kid. Lord, you just never know with them.

Tiffany

All of you let that brat touch me. How humiliating. She shoots out of nowhere. Like the devil she is. All of you acted like we had done something wrong.

Goes to show you can't ever depend on those people to act right in public. You can try dressing them up, but for anything else, there is no accounting.

All I can say is she was very lucky I am such a fair-minded person. I held back. Because of my position, of course. It's like my mother counseled: when you're as beautiful as I am, you have to expect jealousy from everyone, State Kids being the most jealous.

Gladys

When I bumped into the four golden girls combing their perfect hair and yakking, I almost walked out of the bathroom.

They were talking about the new gal in class. The State Kid. Tearing her apart. Just like they had done to me when I was new. Friendly until they found out I wouldn't do their class assignments for them. Smartest kid in the class was no dummy.

But they were gossiping about the new gal. I told them they sounded like they were jealous of her. I was taken off guard. Tiffany pushed me into the corner before I knew what was happening. I thought I was going to die when Jewel shoots out of the stall and surprises us all. Before Tiffany could finish swinging her fist at my face, Jewel grabbed her arm and twisted it behind her back. Tiffany swung her purse and hit Jewel on the head. She swung her purse at me when Jewel punched her in the face. You'd think, with all the shrieking and hollering they were doing, their virtue was in jeopardy. If they have any virtue left.

I tried to tell the teacher who came in that it wasn't Jewel's fault. But nobody listens to the nerd. I heard though. Jewel was in detention for a long time. Too bad no one else will know.

Joylene

Like it was just so totally gross and all. How were we supposed to know? I mean, how do you expect us to react. Ladies do not take swings at each other. Tiffany was forced to do what she did. Like we were just so ultimately amazed, we just stood and watched. Totally paralyzed.

Stephanie

We saw her come out. Everyone talking. About people we knew. It's not like it was her business. Ladies don't swing at each other. Tiffany had to defend herself. Everyone knows. We told them.

Desiree

Goodness, vengeance is God's work. Tiffany was forced to defend herself. God Almighty, you didn't expect me to jump in. We screamed for help. Lord knows that was the right thing to do. I could never stoop to hit anyone. That would be so un-Christian.

Tiffany

All of you are so stupid. My face is completely disfigured. I won't be able to go out of the house for a whole month. The doctor announced there might be permanent damage. None of you have any idea how much I'm suffering.

Debbie

I was the school bathroom monitor that day. I sneaked out for a smoke when I saw those four walk in. Didn't expect any trouble from them. At least, not the kind I can write them up for. When I heard Gladys shriek, I rushed back in. The State Kid had been sitting in one of the stalls and heard everything they said about her.

I have to give the kid credit. Anyone else would have walked out and let those reigning slime queens get away with what they were doing. From what I could tell, she got into a fracas with the regal one. The State Kid bashed her hard with a right. Tiffany's eye was closed for a good week. Tiffany never looked so fine.

I felt bad having to report Jewel. I would have rather given the kid a medal. However, those other three gossip queens were screaming and shouting so much, one of the teachers came in to find out what was going on. Everyone knows. You don't upset the students whose parents have money. So Tiffany received all the attention and sympathy. But for all that, Jewel didn't have a scratch on her, which didn't work well for the kid to get any understanding.

Yet, I have to give credit where credit is due, and the State Kid earned hers. She held her own.

Joylene

Like it's really awesome. Everyone at school is being so nice to Tiffany. Like no one even mentions her eye. How absolutely totally amazing!

Stephanie

Everyone is being so sympathetic. We knew right was on our side. Everyone appreciates us. We told them.

Desiree

God, you'd never believe the people coming up in school and at the ice-cream shop and talking to us. Especially to Tiffany.

Tiffany

All of you know I am suffering so badly. But I have my image to think of. I have to maintain a certain level of nobility over this anguish.

Wasted Girls
by Jewel

Some girls think they have plenty.
They pretend the nasty stuff about being a female isn't about
   them.

Growing up a girl is hearing about all the messes females are.
The messes we do to men.
The curse that happens between our legs.
Things we aren't able to do.
Thoughts we aren't allowed to have.
Thinking ability we aren't allowed to reach.
Bad enough most of us believe these lies.

Being female has no power, some proclaim.
Power comes in the fist of men for now.
Yet the men are learning. They share when they
get the need for what we bring into the mix.

Being a female is a privilege.
Female ears listen with heart.
Females soothe with soul.
Men can do the same.
They have no permission to do so.
They thump their chests and yell that they know best.
They'll protect us from other men just like themselves,
pretending to be different to get the soothing we bring.

Rule #36
Talking is easier than feeling

Grace prays she isn't ticketed as she rolls through another stop sign. She checks her watch—2:45. She still has another five miles to go. Glen would have reserved a table for two in the corner of the dining area, giving them as much intimacy and quiet as could be marshaled in a restaurant.

She eases up on the gas. A slow-moving car pulls in front. She shouldn't take the time to meet Glen, but things have been building up for a while now. If she doesn't pay attention to what's bothering him, she may lose everything. Her heart couldn't take another loss.

Grace overtakes the slow-moving car, passes across double yellow lines, and darts through the intersection.

At the restaurant, she drives up and down the parking lot, searching for a space and locates Glen's car. Oh good, he's still here. She hasn't missed him. She loosens her grip and is surprised at the imprints of her sweaty hands on the steering wheel.

The small lot is full. Anxious to find parking, she drives out into the street next to the restaurant.

She rounds the corner and spots a place opening up. She flips on her turning signal and taps the steering wheel with her fingernails. The driver goes forward a few inches and backs up a few more to maneuver his way out from between the two cars.

She stretches to see past the car, checking for another empty space ahead. There's none.

Grace has decided to get out and help the driver move out from between the two cars, when she hears a loud thud. The departing driver ignores the dent he made on the parked car, jerks forward, and drives up the street, never looking back.

Grace does her best impersonation of parallel parking and leaves most of the car sticking out in the road. She hurries up the sidewalk.

From a block away, she spies a man leave the restaurant. She suspects it's Glen from the easy way he moves his lean body. The man speaks to the doorman, then strolls into the parking lot. She runs across the street, reaches the corner, and yells, "Glen, stop."

By this time, he has reached his car. It is Glen. He bends his long legs and slips into the driver's seat.

The doorman walks back to the stand and looks up when he hears Grace shout. The doorman turns and moves quickly toward the car. Glen pulls out of the lot and heads down the street, away from them. The doorman jogs a few steps after the car but fails to attract Glen's attention.

Grace steps onto the pickup area under the canopy, waving both arms in the air. A car honks, waiting to pull in to drop off passengers.

Grace steps back onto the curb and watches the corner where the taillights of Glen's car disappeared. If she stares hard enough, maybe he'll receive her signal and turn back. After several seconds, she reaches into her handbag and opens her cell phone. "Husband," she tells the computer voice.

She listens to the chirping, then the ringing. The phone voice reports that Glen's phone is turned off.

Her beeper goes off.

Wasted Direction
by Jewel

Notice how sometimes we get lost?
I wonder who was the first to push us off the path from
  ourselves.
It's easy to blame the moms and the dads.
Most times they're on the wrong path themselves.
Someone pushed them off when they were young.

This path has to be right in front of their noses,
we've been told.
We trip over it more times than we think.

Some call this path the way to salvation.
Those with Ph.D.'s call it "actualizing."
It's all the same.

You have to know who and where you are
without the slime put on you by everyone else.
Many see what they choose to see in you,
too afraid to see it in themselves.

Rule #37
Listening well counts

Raúl Ortega walks into his home, seeks out his son, and finds him in the kitchen.

Julián sits at the table and, with his left hand, holds a large geography book open in front of him. A tall glass of milk and a plate with a half-eaten peanut butter and jelly sandwich sits next to the book.

Raúl opens the refrigerator and examines the various offerings. He removes a pitcher of orange juice and gets a glass from the cabinet.

"Got some news today. Thought it might interest you."

A grunt comes from behind the book.

"That girl with Ronnie. The one with the weird hair, she was in a fight today." He pours the orange juice into the glass. "Right on school grounds. Not too smart, if you ask me."

Raúl leans against the counter, seeing only the top of his son's black hair over the top edge of the geography book. Raúl inspects the cover of the book as if he could penetrate it to his son's expression. "Her social worker was notified. Did you hear she has a social worker?"

Julián's hand appears and gropes for the glass. Another grunt comes from behind the book. The glass disappears for a few seconds and reappears with less milk in it.

"I've met up with a lot of State Kids before, but I've never met one itching for trouble like this one."

The glass of milk vanishes and reappears.

"Anyone who associates with her is doomed. Bound to have trouble. No doubt."

He watches for any signs of life, but the book remains impenetrable. "How's Ronnie? Doing okay?"

"Yes, sir."

"Is he still messing with the State Kid?"

"Yup." The sandwich is picked up and returned.

"I've always liked Ronnie. How long have we known him? Since you two were in grade school. Thought the kid had a good head on his shoulders. Never thought he'd mess up his life this way."

A hand appears above the book and turns a page.

"Well, I bet his parents have a lot to say about the girl he's keeping company with." Raúl drains his glass. "Has Ronnie told you anything about her?"

"No, sir." The sandwich disappears behind the book.

"I know how guys share information about girls." Raúl sets his glass on the counter. "I guess you must get an earful from your buddy?"

"Nope." The glass disappears and comes back empty.

Raúl leans against the counter and watches the lump of humanity who resembles his son before an alien possessed him when he became a teen. "I guess you know by now, she's nothing but trouble."

"Yes, sir." A page is turned.

Raúl dusts off his hands and walks out of the kitchen.

In the living room, Raúl does a turnabout, pushes the swinging kitchen door open, and steps back into the kitchen. "When I talk to you, I, at least, expect you to look at me."

He leans over the kitchen table, snatches the book from his son's hand, and drops it on the table with a thud; the plate bounces.

Raúl stares at his son, the long awaited heir who holds all his dreams, his hopes, and his ambitions for the future. "What happened?" He aims his finger at his son's bruised face.

"It doesn't hurt." Julián carries his plate and glass to the kitchen sink.

"I didn't ask you if it hurt . . ."

"I got in a fight." Julián's right eye is swollen shut. The discoloration flowers over his cheek.

"Thank you for telling me the obvious. Now tell me what I want to know."

Julián crosses his arms. "You're not going to ask me if I'm all right?"

"You're standing in front of me, breathing. Tell me."

"Some guys ganged up on Ronnie." Julián rinses his plate and glass and puts them into the dishwasher.

"You had to get into it?"

Julián leans his head forward and eyeballs his father, then lets out a breath and looks at the ceiling. "Cheez."

Raúl steps closer to his son, shooting his finger at him. "What did the principal have to say? Were the cops called?"

"Didn't happen on the school grounds. Are you happy?" Julián turns to walk around his dad.

Raúl halts his son with a hand on his shoulder. "What caused it?"

Julián digs his hands into his pants pockets and mumbles.

"Speak up."

"'Cause of Jewel."

"That State Kid?" Raúl stumbles back a step.

"Ronnie and Jewel were walking to the library. To study. Like they've been doing all along. These guys followed them and called her a name. Ronnie took a swing, and the three of them jumped him." Julián pushes the kitchen door and passes through, saying, "I had to help. I couldn't just not help."

Raúl follows his son out of the kitchen into the living room. "What'd they call her?"

Julián stops with one foot on the first step of the staircase. He stares until he senses his father's impatience and answers, "State Kid."

"Oh."

Raúl sits in the recliner and watches his son disappear up the stairs. He remembers the girl with old eyes that stared at him from the back seat of the squad car when he picked her up for shoplifting. Such sad old eyes.

Wasted Energy
by Jewel

No one has ever fought for me before,
surprised the heck out of me.

I've been called names all my life.
Names are like mirrors.
Projecting myself through the words.
I'm not a slut; I'm left feeling like one.

I feel weird.
Strange.
Someone can defend me?
Don't know what this means.
I can hold my own.
I fight alone.

Rule #38
Holiday season is about giving

"Can you believe it? Julián comes to me and tells me that a bunch of his friends want to come over after Thanksgiving dinner and bring that foster kid we put in jail," says Raúl Ortega.

Marco, Ortega's rookie partner, sighs. He looks through the passenger window of the squad car at the activity on the street. Nothing sidetracks Raúl from the subject he's lecturing about at the moment, even while they're driving around on patrol.

"His friends belong to this student organization called La Raza something or the other. Goodness sake, they need to concentrate on getting high grades to be accepted into a good college instead of waving flags. America is their country."

Marco cringes. He can't tell his senior partner to stop talking. Yet, Raúl's face is five different shades of red. He's going to have a heart attack.

"They want to celebrate something they did with a newsletter." Raúl glares at a group of jacketed young men standing on the corner. "My kid better stay out of trouble at school. The last thing I need is for some teacher to call." He pauses. "That foster kid. Of all the people for him to bring under my roof."

Marco nods. Ortega's uniform is always as stiff and perfect as his attitudes on success.

"Maybe your son thinks he can straighten her out."

"Yeah, like my brother. Dated that white girl and lost everything."

181

Marco shakes his head. "Isn't he head manager at some big Office Depot store?"

"A dead-end job. Where does he go from there? Works eighty-hour weeks. His family life is a wreck."

"He looked okay at the cookout a few weeks ago."

"What do you expect? For him to admit he did the wrong thing by marrying that girl when she said it was his baby. I never believed her. That's why when Julián came to me and asked, I couldn't believe my ears. How could he think I would allow that kid, of all people, in my home?"

The rookie looks out the cruiser's window. Please, let us come across a crime in progress. A jaywalker. Anything.

"Remember I told you about the incident last week?"

Marco hasn't heard about anything else but. "Yeah, something about your son being in a fight and getting a black eye."

"And it was because of her. Just like with my brother."

Marco rolls his eyes. Please God, let this be short.

But his prayers are road-killed as Ortega continues. "For all I know, the kid has ruined my son's reputation, then expects to be invited to Thanksgiving dinner?"

The rookie rubs his forehead. He settles back into the seat to get comfortable. "Earlier, you said they were coming after dinner." A car cuts in front of them, and Marco flinches at the near miss.

Not even traffic distracts his partner. "Doesn't matter. What matters is being seen with a known felon."

"Wasn't it shoplifting?"

"This puny girl isn't going to distract him or maneuver him in the wrong direction. I'm firm about one thing: he's going to get a good education, even if it kills me." Ortega stares out the window and sighs. "Listen, I know I can't control my kid's life all the time, but . . ."

"But your son is a good kid, and he takes after his father. He'll make the right choices."

Ortega scowls, eyebrows meeting in the middle. "Kids have no real concept of the future."

Marco nods. His partner works at what he's talking about. Many a time, a book on some aspect of career building or professional development sits on the seat between them.

"But after that scene at the school, I have to admit the foster girl has spunk. She doesn't back down from nothing."

Marco grins to the window as he remembers Ortega recounting the incident to him. "Seems to me, if you try to interfere, it might make her look more desirable to him." Marco spots a car jerking its way through a stop sign. "Something like Romeo and Juliet." He flips on the flashing lights.

Raúl steers the cruiser around the car ahead of them, turns the corner, and speeds after the offending driver. "Hey, this is my kid you're talking about. He's not that stupid."

Marco rubs his forehead.

Rule #39
Holidays are for the people that count

Holiday dinner is kind of screwy. Foster mom's family arrives with foil-covered dishes. The men move in front of the football game on television, and the women gravitate to the kitchen, the place for gossip. A couple of hours and several complaints from the living room later, everyone scrambles to the table to eat and check out the new foster kid. Everybody sits around, nodding at one another. Big smiles are plastered on their faces. Dentures just back from the cleaners. Everyone's checking out the others.

Jewel sits at the table, chomping on her food like everyone else. She listens to family members talk about all kinds of folks with names that aren't familiar to her. Jewel is supposed to show how grateful she is for being included in someone else's family.

They speak as if Jewel can't hear.

"The child looks like such a sweetheart. What could she have done to be put in foster care?"

Jewel wants to say, killed a man. Robbed a bank. Stole my mother's lover. Pick one.

"She seems to have good manners."

Just learned how to eat with a fork. Courtesy of the State Agency. Real nice folks. They broke my fingers teaching me.

"For a foster child, she doesn't appear frightfully abnormal."

Ain't seen anything yet. Wait until I tell you how big it was. This big. Why, my mother's boyfriend's penis, of course.

"I'm sure that after a while in your care, she'll be just fine."

When my own mother washed the dishes after the big holiday dinner like this one, I was the best dessert my mother's boyfriend ever had. Told me so. Can I have seconds, please?

"The foster child's so quiet. Doesn't she ever say anything?"

My mother hopes I have a daughter as malicious and as ungrateful as I've been to her. If I make my daughter dessert so I don't have to hold a job, then I pray my daughter's a bitch and fights back.

"Just ignore her. She does it for the attention."

Everyone shovels in all they can, like they have a time limit on how much they can eat.

"Fresh coffee. Pie anyone?"

"Why, thank you so very much," Jewel says right through her big all-tooth smile.

The world is nothing without good manners.

Rule #40
To want something is to make it go away

The social worker sits at a student desk in Jewel's homeroom. She scrutinizes the man in front of her. Tom Garner's appearance favors a model's more than a schoolteacher. Tall and slim, he wears a crisp blue shirt with a darker blue silk tie, knotted at his neck. His brown eyes are clear and, at the moment, full of laughter.

Tom asks, "Would you like to check my credentials?"

Grace looks puzzled at him. "What?"

"My credentials. I have them here." He points to the top of his desk.

Grace clears her throat. "Mr. Garner, I appreciate your seeing me when the counselor wasn't available, but I'm not sure what your role is or what you have to contribute."

"Right."

Tom pulls his desk chair out and around his desk, steering it with one hand, and stops it close to where Grace sits.

"I've worked with Jewel a lot lately." He sits down. "She's coming along. Considering."

"That's quite a huge 'considering,' Mr. Garner. The reports I received state something quite opposite. She was in a fight with a girl in the restroom."

"I spoke with the young lady that was the bathroom monitor that day. The final story was a bit different than the actual event."

"You're saying because she's the State Kid, she received the short end of the stick?"

"Right, but . . ."

"What about the fight some boys had in front of the library? It was reported that a police officer's son was involved in that melee."

"Well, actually that was good."

"Good?"

"It gave Jewel an idea of how it feels to have someone defend her."

Grace straightens up quickly, concern on her face. "Were any of the boys assaulting her?"

"Only if you think being called a 'State Kid' is being assaulted."

"Jewel has to learn to solve complications in her life in a more civilized manner."

"Yeah, but sometimes life isn't so civilized to you."

"My reports confirm that after school Jewel's been going to some boy's apartment, where a whole crowd of skinheads hang out. The foster mother stated that Jewel has come home drunk several times."

"Yes, I was worried about that, too. But I gave her the assignment to tutor this young man, and I've noticed lately that she's been with that crowd instead."

"This is the crowd that fought?"

"Well, uh, kind of." Tom rubs the back of his neck.

Grace glares at the teacher, then arranges her jacket. "I'm going to remove Jewel from this school and enroll her in an alternate educational placement." Grace scratches her nose at the scent of chalk on the teacher's hands. "I feel she needs more one-on-one supervision. I believe with the right motivation, she could go far."

"You can say something like that about *any* kid."

"I'm speaking about Jewel right now."

"Jewel's slick. She has a lot on the ball. To move her would be a mistake."

"I appreciate your efforts at evaluation, Mr. Garner . . ."

"But I don't know shit from shinola."

Grace looks up from her file. "Excuse me?"

Tom leans forward, elbows on knees. "I'm only a teacher."

Grace goes back to her file. "Next week, I plan to enroll Jewel in an alternate school environment and will move her to a new foster home. She needs stability."

"That would be a mistake."

"A mistake? How?"

"You really don't know Jewel, do you?"

Grace clutches the file to her chest. "Excuse me?"

"Have you taken the time to connect with Jewel? Really know her. I mean," he points at the file she holds, "more than what you read in there?"

"I don't perceive any benefits for Jewel in discussing our relationship with you." Grace stands with a cactus-straight spine.

"Don't get me wrong." Tom stands up, several inches taller than the social worker. Grace looks up at him. "I take into account how you social workers are so bogged down in paperwork; your workloads are unmanageable."

"But?" Grace holds her head up, shoulder muscles tightening.

"Jewel's doing well. She's making friends. Only positive things can come from this."

"Yes, friendships are good. I agree. But the friendships here don't seem to be heading her in the right direction." Grace moves to the front of the room as Tom sits back in his chair and watches her.

"But she has friends. Her own age. I bet that's something new for her."

"Well, yes, I suppose you could say that."

"Are you aware that the kid's quite brilliant?"

Astonishment replaces Grace's professional face.

"She thinks a lot. To herself. That's good and . . ."

"No." Grace shakes her head. "That's bad . . ."

"And good," Tom says. "I just had a meeting where everyone showed me pieces of her work. She's getting A's in all her classes, but she doesn't let on to anyone her own age."

"This meeting? Why was it called?" Grace clutches her briefcase.

"The math teacher had concerns about my assigning Jewel as a tutor."

"His main concern being . . ."

"That as a State Kid she might do more harm than good."

Grace moves. The teacher's desk is between them. "And wherever I move Jewel, she's going to be a State Kid."

"Right. Here, she's ahead of the game because she's doing well in all her classes. As bright as she is, she's doing good probably because it's so easy and it's boring."

Graces leans against the teacher's desk. "Jewel doesn't realize she's doing so well because she's involved with this tutoring assignment."

Tom steps in front of Grace. "Exactly. I think that we can slip in some normalcy into her life without her knowing it."

With a finger, Grace follows the groove on the desk as she ponders his information. Stability is good. She remembers never unpacking because some other relative would have a need for her at some point. Jewel never mentioned friends to her; she did talk about that stupid boy, as she called him, she was tutoring. All her conversations were focused on how great the visits were with her mother. She could use friends.

"Okay, I like your plan. But," she raises a hand, "we're going to do this as long as you can prove to me that something positive is happening."

Tom salutes. "Yes, ma'am. You're in charge at all times."

Wasted Wanting
by Jewel

Trust is important to living.
This teacher wants to teach me about trust.
Who is he fooling?

Never met a man totally safe.
Never met a man who didn't have but one action on his mind.

This teacher is different.
Talks old.
Is going bald.
Acts gentle.

Gentle can break a dam.
Because one gentle touch feels good,
making you want more.

Forget how gentle feels.
It is tough to be strong.

Rule #41
Love is grand

Two more days and Ronnie will take the big scholarship exam. Everybody knows about the test. All the students cheer him on. The librarian offers him a thumbs-up when he and Jewel walk in.

"You getting antsy about the test coming up?"

"Nah, I'll do fine. You're one good teacher."

Jewel smiles. "So, what making the chair so hot, you not sitting still."

"Listen, Jewel . . ."

"Here comes the excuses." Jewel whispers across the table in the library. She doesn't want to attract attention because the librarian had commented on how unladylike her red-plaid shirt with holes in the elbows, paint-splattered jeans, and her high tops with no shoelaces were. She pointed out that Jewel could take lessons from Ronnie on how to dress properly and behave appropriately.

Ronnie had grinned and said, "Yeah, I'm sophisticated." The older woman walked away smiling with the bright bulb on.

Now the librarian squints over in their direction and snorts disapprovingly at Jewel. She nods at Ronnie and mouths, "You're going to go far, young man."

Ronnie waves at her, chuckles, and says to Jewel, "You know me like no one else does."

Jewel pinches her arm under the table. "So, what you fish-hooking me for with all the honey talk?"

"I need to go somewhere. If I promise to study an extra hour in the morning, would you mind if I left early?" He cocks his head to one side and winks at her.

"I not mind. What going on?"

"Nothing much. I made somebody a promise I'd show up at a dress rehearsal. There's this big play being put on by the drama club just before we're let out for Christmas. Heard about it?"

Jewel nods. She sits up straighter and runs her hand through her uncombed red-painted hair.

"Today's dress rehearsal, and I promised I'd show up for support. Guess I'm learning how to be a sensitive guy from hanging with you." Ronnie laughs, and several heads turn in their direction.

"This play happening when?"

"The Friday night before we're let out. Find out if you're going to be free."

"This play, it of interest to go?"

"Yeah, I think so. It's some spectacular event from what I've been told." Ronnie uses his arm to slide all the books from the table into his backpack. "I have the inside scoop about the production. I can tell you all about it later if you want. But things like a play don't interest you."

"Not tell me what I think. I like all sorts of stuff. You not know all."

"Really? Let's go. It'll be lots of fun."

"I not have any clothes super-fine for a night out."

Ronnie adjusts the books in his pack. "Jewel, you always look just fine."

"I get a dress from one of the other girls I live with."

"Why bother? No one would recognize you if you came any different."

"I like dressing nice some time."

Ronnie zips up his backpack. "You would look great, I bet. It'd be awesome to have you come to the play."

Jewel leans forward. "I would very much like to go with . . ."

A soft voice plops between them like a balloon full of water: "Ronnie, are you ready yet?"

Ronnie is on his feet in a flash with a smile so big it makes his ears stick out.

"Hi, Marisela. This is my pal, Jewel. The one I've told you all about." His adoration radiates from his face and blanks out the overhead lights.

Marisela, in a tight, long-sleeved, black knit mini dress, smiles at Jewel. "You must be very smart to be so much help to my Ronnie. Everyone appreciates all the work you've done with him." She looks up at her boyfriend. "Chulo, I have to be on time. Are you coming with me?"

Ronnie looks at Jewel.

"Not listen to me. It your own life you messing."

Ronnie sits down, alarmed at her attitude. "What's with you?"

"Nothing. Just go. People waiting for your butt." Jewel turns her head away.

Ronnie reaches across the table with an open hand. "I'll see you tomorrow." His hand remains empty.

Marisela wraps her hands around Ronnie's arm. "Chulo, I'm going to be late." She swings a delicate hand over to Jewel. "Please come to the play. It would mean a lot to Ronnie. I'll save you a seat in the front, next to Ronnie. You can come with us to the cast party afterwards." She smiles the star-of-the-show smile.

"Probably."

Ronnie jumps up, forgetting his forgotten hand and slings his backpack across his shoulder. "Great! Let's go. Everyone is waiting for the award-winning actor of the whole play."

They walk away, arm in arm. Ronnie bends his head down to listen to Marisela, who is slender and beautiful even from behind. Her head dips as she tells him the news, hands around Ronnie's arm.

They are a couple. They walk out of the library, and all the patrons gaze after them with smiles on their faces.

Wasted Love
by Jewel

I'm stupid.
Plain stupid.
Ronnie is just a boy,
a stupid boy with red cheeks, flapping lips, eyes blinking.
In love with that beautiful girl.
He calls me a friend.
Says I'm pretty.
I'm not so dumb as to get fishhooked by those falsehoods.
I'm too smart for idiot stuff like soft feelings.
Mom believes that love's the cure for everything.
"Love" has caused her pain all of her life.

Love never brings anything except pain.
I'm way too smart to volunteer to get whacked upside
  the head.
I was doing spectacular fine before his time.
I'll do stupendous fine with him gone.
I won't roughen my knees for him.

Rule #42
Never give your heart,
the exchange window is always open

"Mom."

Nothing.

"Mom, you home?"

Quiet.

I walk through my mom's house. On the coffee table, I count five empty beer bottles. They're not the brand she likes. I hope her latest isn't here.

In the kitchen, everything sparkles. My mom likes everything super clean. She works hard for the house to look polished.

I check the backyard, then I go through the kitchen and living room and head to the bedrooms. Maybe my mom is at the mall.

"Mom?"

I have to talk to her about Ronnie and Marisela. She will understand. She will say the right thing to make the pain go away. And I have to talk to her before the social worker finds out I'm there without permission.

My mom's bedroom door is closed. I put my ear to the door to be certain I'm interrupting any romping in bed. Silence.

I tap on the door.

"Mom? You there?"

Where else can she be?

I twist the doorknob, and the door swings open.

"Mom?" I stick my head in the room.

The room is night dark. The heavy blue curtains are shut across the windows. The air is thick and stale. My mom is just at the mall. That's it.

My eyes adjust; the dark is so deep.

I walk in, pull the curtains open, and look around the room. Clothes everywhere. A suitcase is open on the floor almost filled with dresses, some half in, others half out.

Mom left? She left without telling me she was leaving? What latest fool talked her into this scheme? Why wouldn't she tell me? She tells me everything. Why not this time?

Maybe she finally got tired of me. She found someone better to take care of her? I tried really hard. I did everything I could. Thought of everything she needed and even of stuff she didn't know she needed. I did a lot for my mom all of the time, so she'd keep loving me. I'm supposed to be the one to take care of her.

If she's gone, what's left for me to do? There'll be no "who" to wonder about me? If I'm alone, who will care if I breathe or not? I'll have no family.

The armchair is turned to the window, an empty vodka bottle lying on the floor next to it. No glass. My mom hasn't left me; my mom's just at the mall.

I move to the middle of the room, dragging my feet. The closet door is open. No hangers on the rod. They're all on the floor.

The heap of blankets on the bed moves. A groan rises from the blankets. I rush to the bed and find my mom. When she rolls over, she smells of sweaty skin and booze.

I touch her face with the back of my hand. I shake her by the shoulder.

She moans and pulls away. She drank all the booze.

With one leg underneath her, I sit on the bed and wonder how long she has been like this. I search the room for signs of any latest and don't find one.

I go to the dresser, several open prescription bottles lie next to the silver-plated hairbrush. All empty.

I dash back to my mother, grab her by both shoulders, and shake her hard. "Mom, wake up."

She shoves my hands away.

"Mom, how long ago did you take the pills?"

She mumbles something about sleep.

I shake her harder; my mother's body moves like a dead puppy. "Mom, you can't die. Wake up."

She opens her eyes and peers out from beneath red-rimmed eyelids. "Is that you, Jewel? You came home. I knew you would. I knew nothing could keep my baby from coming back to take care of her mommy."

"Mom, you got to wake up." I pull her up into a sitting position.

My mom puts a cold hand to my face. "My baby. The best thing that ever happened to me." Tears flood her speech, and she gulps. "I let you down. I always let you down."

"No, you didn't, Mom."

"I let everyone down. I'm no good." She falls back on the bed. "Everything's too hard." She pulls the blankets over her head.

I whip the blankets out of her hand. "Mom, how long ago did you take the pills?"

She squints. "Pills?"

"Yes, Mom. The pills. How long ago?"

"Let me sleep." She turns and pushes me away.

I jump from the bed and run into the bathroom. I yank the medicine cabinet open and go through the shelves of bottles, dropping several into the lavatory. I find the bottle I'm looking for.

I sprint into the kitchen, fill a glass with water, yank the drawer open, and grab a spoon. I snatch up a wastebasket from the hallway as I hustle back into my mom's bedroom.

I drop the wastebasket next to the bed and set bottle, spoon, and glass on the nightstand. "Mom, you have to help me. You have to sit up."

"I'm no help. Just no good."

I slip my arm underneath her shoulders. "C'mon, Mom, sit up." I heave her into a sitting position and stuff pillows behind her back. She slumps onto the pillows.

I take the bottle and pour Ipecac in the spoon. "Mom, open your mouth."

She shakes her head.

I put the bottle back down and pinch her nose shut. She opens her mouth, and I stick in the spoon and pour the liquid down her throat.

She sputters and chokes; some of the medicine dribbles down her chin. "Tastes awful."

I pour another spoonful down her throat. "Mom, hold this." I take her right hand, then her left, and wrap them around the wastebasket. "Vomit into this. I'm going to make some coffee."

The coffee's almost done when I hear her throwing up.

I walk back into her bedroom with a mug in one hand and the coffeepot in the other. I stand next to the bed and wrinkle my nose from the sour stench of the vomit.

She vomits all over herself and down the side of the bed. The wastebasket lies on the other side of her.

I set the pot and mug down, push the wastebasket off the bed, and peel off the covers.

"It's cold," she complains.

"You have to sit over here, so I can clean you up."

I coax her off the bed. With a foot and one hand, I turn the armchair around and help her into the chair.

"Drink this." I hand her a mug full of hot coffee.

She waves it away.

"If you don't drink it, I'll hold your nose again."

She glares and takes the mug.

"Drink."

Like a little child, she sips. "I tried really hard to be a good mother to you." She talks into her cup. "I tried really hard."

I tip the cup to her mouth. "I know, Mom."

"When you were little, I was with Devonne. Or was it Jeffery?"

I turn away and go through the dresser drawers and find another nightgown. I've heard these stories plenty of times already.

"You were crying in your crib. Nothing I did would stop your crying. I felt scared. My boyfriend said your crying irritated him."

I wet a washcloth with warm water in the bathroom.

"I wanted you to stop crying really badly. I stuffed a bottle in your mouth. I switched your clean diaper for another. You spit back the food I fed you. You kept crying. Nothing I did could quiet you down."

I wipe her face.

"I could hear him going through my purse. Grocery money was all I had. He yelled at me to quiet the baby because he couldn't hear the television."

I struggle to pull the dirty nightgown off, her weight resting against my shoulders.

"I patted you on your back. Walked you up and down the room. I put you back in the crib because I could feel my hand turning into a fist. The fist was too close to your body. I pulled the fist away with my other hand. I held the fist tight to my chest. I cursed you. I cursed myself. I cursed the pill I forgot to take. I cursed the job that kept me so tired."

I wipe her arms and chest with the warm cloth. Her nakedness is familiar from previous times.

"I screamed at you to shut up. I felt my fist growing stronger. My fist was so near your head. It frightened me. I ran out of the room and locked myself in the bathroom."

Every few moments, I urge her to take another sip of coffee.

"Inside the bathroom, I sat on the floor. I squashed myself into the corner, held my fist against my chest, and breathed big gulps of air. I prayed the fist would get smaller and would go back into its cage. Because I didn't want to hurt you. I didn't ever, ever want to hurt you.

"I heard my boyfriend walk by the bathroom door. I heard him yell at you to shut up. I heard him hit you, even when I covered my ears."

I slip the clean nightgown on over her head and work it down below her waist.

"When it was quiet and I came out, I took care of the bruises. I changed your diaper and rocked you until my boyfriend came back. He wanted me. I knew things would be okay as long as he wanted me."

I shift on my knees, when her hand strikes out and grips my arm. The flesh turns white around her fingers.

"I never hit you. I never ever hit you. Never even once when you were growing up."

"I believe you, Mom." I pry her fingers loose. "I believe you."

A gurgle, and she vomits all over herself again. She cries.

I call 911 and give the calm voice the address.

I ease my mom to her feet, walk her into the bathroom, and stick her in the shower. I turn on the water, and she sputters and chokes as I hold her under the water until she's clean. One-handed, I find another nightgown in the hamper and sit her back into the armchair. I strip the bed and make it up with clean sheets. I put her back to bed and tuck the sheet under her chin.

"Evil spirits away with you. Only angels and good fairies visit my mother tonight."

My mom smiles.

I stand completely still until her breaths are regular.

I rush to answer the doorbell. A paramedic comes in and takes my mother's vital signs. Another collects the empty prescription bottles on the dresser. "Why didn't you call us right away? This isn't a game."

"Leave the kid alone," the stocky man says. "She did all the right things."

The taller of the two replies, "Yeah, lucky."

The stocky man snaps his bag shut. "Nothing to do with luck." He points to my mother. "This one's a habitual. Kid's been taking care of her for a long time now."

The taller man gawks at Mom. "You know her?"

The stocky man nods and looks at me. "The usual routine. Your mom will be hospitalized overnight. You can come and get her tomorrow."

I don't say a word. I stand very still and watch them roll my mom out and into the ambulance. I close the door after they go.

In my mom's bedroom, I drag the armchair around to face the window. I sink into the cushions, look out the window, and try hard to visualize what my mother saw, try really hard to understand what she fears.

I pick up the pad of paper from the windowsill. "Dear Jewel" was written across the top. At least she was going to say good-bye. I rip the page off, crumble it one-handed, and let it drop to the floor.

Wasted Death
by Jewel

My mom's wanting to die
has more to do with her wanting to live.

There is no living without hope.

Dying isn't something most people want to talk about.
But for some, like my mom, death can be a place to rest.

Dying is a way of running away from things too weighty.
None of us can tell another person how much is too much.

There is no living without hope.

I want my mom to live.
But long ago I caught on to why she wants to turn off the
    pain.
I understand, and sometimes,
recognize the load she struggles under.
I'm not ready to let her go.

There is no living without hope.

Some think that to die by your own hand is selfish.
You think all that's needed is putting on a smiley face?
Pulling yourself up by your own bootstraps?
A person who feels she makes no impression on the world,
makes no difference in others' lives,
makes no difference in her own life,
has no hope.

The disease of suicide is not being able to see or feel the
    hope.

Rule #43
Never underestimate hate

The next day, Jewel peers at the two figures with shoulders as wide as car seats, and they are walking toward her.

"Nice babe," says one.

"New bod's more important," says the other one standing next to the first voice.

Jewel identifies the sound of lust. She works to get up but has been drinking since morning. She skipped school and, along with her classmate Deano, found her way to this apartment.

Most of the day, there have been three or four guys in the one-bedroom apartment. In the living room, Jewel slouches on the ripped sofa. A chair with a cushion missing is next to a small T.V. on a crate. Next to the window, a wobbly card table with four mismatched chairs sits in the corner, where guys join and leave the ongoing poker game. The kitchen window has bars across it. All the refrigerator holds is beer. A stiff mold-covered loaf of bread sits on the counter, open. A boom box is plugged in, heavy metal blaring.

A heap of empty beer cans grows against the wall beside the door. The walls are gray with paint falling off in large flakes. The only light fixture in the living room has been replaced with a fluorescent blue light that sizzles like a signal from outer space. Now, as it grows dark outside, six guys play poker, and the television's loud, but no one watches.

The bald one sits next to her and strokes her arm. "Fresh flesh. No one told us it was banquet night."

Jewel smells the sweat from his body and jerks her arm away. "I my own person. I ride free."

The one standing, who wears a blue T-shirt with the sleeves ripped off, laughs. "No one with a wound like yours rides free." He leans over her and blocks out the view of the whole apartment.

Deano comes up behind him. "Hey, she's from my school. She's not for public use." He sways, a beer in his hand.

Blue T-shirt reaches around him and shoves Deano away. "Go watch television. This is a man's game."

Jewel stands up. The bald man grabs the back of her jeans and pulls her down on him.

They both laugh as she protests. "Scumbags, let me go."

The guys playing poker nudge each other to check out the scene.

Deano approaches them again. "Let her go. She's mine."

The bald one wraps his arm around Jewel and cups her crotch with his hand. "Wounds like this are for public use." He grabs Jewel's arm and pins it down.

Deano shoves himself on the man standing. "Wait . . ."

Blue T-shirt twists at the waist, bringing his arm around, and backhands the boy.

Deano flies across the room, bangs his head against the wall, and lands on the pile of empty beer cans, unconscious.

One or two faces check out the empties rolling across the floor, then go back to their card game.

The bald man spits into Jewel's ear.

Blue T-shirt unzips her jeans and pulls them down.

Jewel twists and turns, swinging her one free arm and clubs the arm of the man holding her.

The bald man bends his head, opens his mouth, and fills it with tender shoulder, biting hard.

Jewel pulls her body down into his and away from his mouth, but his bite on her flesh remains firm. He shakes his head like a puppy with a sock in his mouth, then lets go. Blood stains her shirt.

"It's not nice to hit. Didn't anyone ever teach you manners?"

Both men laugh.

The boys who were playing cards are now paying attention to the two men with Jewel. One of them at the table grins and rubs his crotch in glee. One downs the rest of his beer and crushes the can with both hands.

Blue T-shirt pulls Jewel's panties down. Blue T-shirt laughs and lets out a howl. "Party time." He unzips his pants.

The boys toss their cards on the makeshift table. They smack their lips in anticipation.

Blue T-shirt pulls himself out of his pants, working his penis into an erection.

Jewel sinks into the man holding her from behind and kicks up both her legs. Her feet land in Blue T-shirt's stomach.

Blue T-shirt doubles over with all the air escaping in a whoosh. He stumbles back a couple of steps.

The group of boys watching cheer and raise their cans and bottles in jubilee.

Blue T-shirt glares them into silence, turns back, and fixes on her a look she knows promises a lot of pain.

She kicks out with her legs.

He grabs her feet and pins them under his arms.

She spits at him. The glob lands on his leg.

Blue T-shirt raises his arm and slaps her with the back of his hand several times on her crotch.

Jewel crams her screams inside and fights to free her legs.

Blue T-shirt punches her in the stomach.

She sinks against the bald man holding her and bites her lip to stop from screaming. Pain fills her body.

The bald man grips her on top of him with one hand, massages her breast through her thin top with the other, rotating his hips up against her butt.

Jewel thrashes around, attempting to wrestle her legs free, and beats on the bald man's arm.

He pinches her breast hard.

She's lifted up into the air with her legs dangling.

The bald man moves from underneath her.

Blue T-shirt drops her back on the sofa, and she feels her legs being split apart.

She twists away from Blue T-shirt.

He puts a hand on her throat. "Be a good girl now."

Blue T-shirt spears her, plunging as far as he can go. "Shit. The cunt's used goods."

Jewel disappears inside of herself where purple feathers protect her.

Wasted Body
by Jewel

I'm going.
Going to the quiet place inside of me,
the place where no one can see me.
My body is getting used, but I'll be free.

My body gets me into trouble all the time.
Don't know why.
Maybe I'm a wound for others to use.

Sometimes I have to breathe their air,
foul and stale, to stay alive. Sometimes
I wonder why I stay alive.

I slip away to the quiet place inside
of me, hiding from the dragon's fire.
I bury myself even lower.

Sometimes I wonder how deep
I have to go before I hit rock.

Sometimes I wonder if
I'll ever come out.

Sometimes I wonder if
anyone will ever rescue me.

Stupid girl.
Wondering is for others.
I'm lost, hidden, ugly.

I'm for nothing.
Or else this wouldn't be happening to me.

Rule #44
Knights come in blue shirts

Loud knocking comes from somewhere far, far on the outside of Jewel.

A pounding on the door is accompanied with a loud "Open the door. Police. Neighbors are complaining about the noise."

Blue T-shirt punches the arm of his buddy. "C'mon. Cops."

The bald man pushes Jewel from under him, off the sofa.

She lands with a thud and a pound of hurt as her head hits the floor.

The boys scramble over each other out the window and run down the fire escape ladder.

The bald man nods his head toward the door, next to the sofa, leading into the bedroom.

Blue T-shirt smiles and glints down at Jewel. "Stupid. Not even worth the hassle." He swings his leg back for a kick when his buddy calls out to him. Blue T-shirt follows the bald man into the bedroom.

One of the boys attempts to join them.

Blue T-shirt fills his hand with the boy's face, pushes him down, and shuts the bedroom door as two police officers come through the front entrance.

One of the officers chases the fallen boy to the window he's climbing through and investigates the fire escape; the other boys run like ants out of a hole in the ground. The officer scrambles out the door into the hallway of the apartment building, yelling into his squawk box for backup.

The other officer stands next to Jewel.

She's curled up into a ball and looks up. "Officer."

Raúl Ortega squats down, noting the bruises on her thighs and the blood between her legs, and shakes his head. He rubs his face with his open hand.

Jewel points to the bedroom door.

A squeak and the bedroom door swings open. Off balance, Raúl Ortega gets to his feet, raising his gun.

Blue T-shirt jumps out with his gun aimed and fires.

Raúl clutches his chest and falls forward. He rolls over onto his back.

Blue T-shirt stands over the officer and takes aim.

Raúl attempts to lift his gun with his left hand.

Jewel braces herself with her arms and kicks Blue T-shirt on the side of his knee.

The shot hits the floor next to Raúl's head.

Blue T-shirt yells, "You stupid bitch," and kicks her in the stomach.

She folds and grips her stomach.

"Let's go before more cops get here," the bald man shouts. "The hallway's clear."

Blue T-shirt leaps after his buddy down the hallway and out of sight.

Jewel crawls over to where Raúl Ortega lies bleeding. She sits next to him and uses her jacket to squelch the flow of blood from his shoulder. "You be all right. You be all right."

"Why weren't you in school today?"

Jewel smiles. "Always the cop. No matters."

He coughs and spits blood. "Julián asked me. Ronnie's been looking for you all day."

"Not matter anyhow."

A clamor begins in the hallway. Raúl Ortega lifts his gun as a group of uniformed men burst into the room.

A couple of the officers race to check on Raúl on the floor. Raúl swings his hand in her direction. "Innocent victim. Take care of her." He passes out.

One of the officers wraps a jacket around Jewel.

Rule #45
Family is good in the long run

Jewel hates hospitals and tries sneaking out twice.

The cops have been nice to her ever since they found out she could identify who shot Ortega.

She sits in the corridor of the hospital after the doctors check her out. The rape crisis counselor sits nearby, wanting to hold her hand, thinking she's going to tell Jewel something she's never heard before.

Julián arrives with his mother. He cups his mother's elbow and helps her to a chair as if she were fragile. He pats her hand as he steps away.

Ronnie and Marisela show up a little later. Ronnie places his hand on Julián's shoulder. Marisela stands close to Julián. They're tight. They have each other to lean on during the bad times.

More family arrives. Men relatives with fat stomachs pat Julián on the back. Women relatives with hankies stuck to their eyes surround Julián's mother. Little kids watch grown-ups act funny.

Someone remembers food. Someone else thinks of a priest. Family. Taking care of each other.

Jewel sits on a hard plastic chair. Even the counselor has left. Best way to be. Easier to slip away. The nurse calls Jewel's name. Cops want to talk to her.

This attracts Ronnie's attention.

Down the hallway away from the group, a cop walks beside her. Ronnie catches up with them and asks the cop if he can speak with Jewel.

The cop quizzes her.

She shakes her head. "I don't know him. No relation. No connection. Ever."

Rule #46
People will always surprise you

The three of them walk into the Elkins' bedroom. One is dressed in ruffles, the other two wear short skirts and tight tops. Their eyes are dark with makeup. Their lips are outlined with a dark color and filled in with a lighter one.

Norma glances from them to Jewel, gets off her bed, and leaves the room.

They stand and stare at Jewel. She stares back. They peek at each other, then inspect her some more.

"We growing old looking at each other?" Jewel asks. She crosses her legs pretzel style.

One of them steps up. The spokesperson. Of course, it had to be her.

"All of us came because . . ."

"Because you hearing what happened and wanting to say how sorry you is. But really, you wanting to check out how I look so you can goes back and tell all your girlfriends about it."

If they're looking for pitiful, Jewel thinks, they're going to have to go far to find it in her.

The spokesperson tilts her head. "Why don't you stop being so smart all the time and let someone help you?"

"Yeah? You volunteering?" Like anyone would want to care for someone who comes from where I come from. The planet rape.

"Yeah, I am," Marisela says.

"Me too," Raquel says and steps even with Marisela.

"And me," Teresa says. She stands behind them.

Jewel probes them, and for the first time ever, she doesn't have words to throw back at them.

Marisela moves closer to the bed. "We want to invite you to the play. It's going to be very special, and we want to make sure you show up."

"Sorry, got no clothes for wearing." Wouldn't be caught dead there anyway. She's nobody's charity case.

Raquel moves up. "Oh, that's no problem. I have lots you can wear."

Jewel measures Raquel's chest, heaving out of her dress, and looks down at her own flat nothing. She laughs. She'll be the joke for everyone.

Marisela says, "We have time to fix it up. My grandmother is good with sewing and stuff like that. She would like you."

"Why?" Like Jewel needs it or wants it. She's never found anyone who likes her for very long.

Marisela ignores Jewel's question. "We have another invitation."

"Yeah, to what?" What do these girls think they are fishhooking her into? She doesn't need to be saved, especially by them. She doesn't need a parade of do-gooders in her life.

"There's this group we belong to. We want you to come with us. It could really help you."

"Like what? Some kind of social club or something? I get to plan dances with all of you, watching while you dance with your boyfriends?"

This is too much. They're earning their Brownie points by being nice to the State Kid. She wants nothing to do with them. They can peddle their salvation to some other sorry mess. She's fine alone.

Raquel moves to the other side of the bed and sits down. "I was fourteen when it happened to me."

Jewel draws back and braces her back against the wall. "Why that meaning anything to me?" Oh no. Now Jewel has to listen to their sad stories. She's had enough of her mother's for a lifetime.

Teresa sits behind Marisela and touches her shoulder.

Jewel stares hard at Marisela. Not her. Not Ronnie's girl.

Marisela looks down and picks at the fluff on the bed. "I was on vacation with my folks. I had gone out with my cousins. I got lost."

"When?" Jewel has to know. Was this before or after Ronnie? Because nothing's supposed to happen when you have a guy who loves you. He's supposed to make everything right in your life. Mom always said this was true.

Marisela hangs her head. Her hands are in fists; she wraps the bedspread around them.

Raquel reaches across the bed and clutches Marisela's hand up from the bedspread. Teresa pats Marisela's shoulder. Jewel's stuck in the middle of this pity party, and she wants no part of it.

Marisela looks at her. "Last month. During Thanksgiving break."

"But, you got Ronnie." Jewel stares at her, and it hits her. "Does he know?"

"I haven't been able to tell him. I'm too scared to." Marisela speaks in a voice not much more than a squeak. Glorious, wonderful, beautiful her.

Jewel gawks at Marisela. Someone as fantastic as she is, is too afraid to tell the boy who loves her. She's perfect. Things like what's been done to Jewel don't happen to people like Marisela. She has a boyfriend. He adores her no matter what. Only people like Jewel do alone.

Raquel takes over. "She has to come to terms with the rape herself. Then she'll bring Ronnie, and someone will teach him how to help. Most of the guys aren't too good with how to handle things like this."

"But Ronnie so goodness . . . he loving you so much." Marisela has the magic answer Angela has looked for all her life. Of course, everything is perfect for Marisela. She never has to feel what alone is.

"Yeah, but guys need help understanding this kind of stuff, too." The three of them stare at Jewel. "That's why we're here. We want you to know you're not alone."

They don't fool Jewel. She does alone best of all. Alone was invented for the likes of her. They think just because they've come, she'll believe they're thinking of her. She's nobody's fool. She's smarter than that. She'll tell them where they can put all their phony good intentions. Right straight into hell.

"Listen, I does fine. You not needing to worry about me. I not needing no thing you got for . . ."

A knock on the door shuts her up. The knotted-tight social worker walks in, stops, and does a double take when she discovers them all on the bed.

Jewel tells the three charity givers, "See? I not all alone." She waves her hand at the uptight social worker. "I having my fairy godmother to take care of me."

The three girls stand up fast and move to one side of the room. Raquel says, "We came to invite Jewel to join our group at the Rape Crisis Center."

"Oh, I was just about to mention it to . . ." The social worker checks Jewel out.

She sits back and polishes her fingernails on her purple-with-yellow-ducks shirt.

Mrs. Clarke turns back to the girls. "No, I'm sorry. I have this other group I think will be much better for Jewel. I picked it out for her myself." She looks at Jewel. "Right now, I have to take you to the hospital for some follow-up on your injuries and a blood test."

"A blood test? Why they using me for a pincushion?" Today, everyone is using her for their test pattern. Sheesh.

Teresa nods as Raquel says, "Checking for HIV."

Jewel acts defiant toward the social worker. "You say you picking this thingy for me?"

The social worker nods. "I think the group I have in mind will be much better for you than the one these young people are recommending."

Jewel catches the look on her face of having made up her mind. "How come I not make this choice myself? This be my life you talking about. How come I not able to go to this place they talk about?"

The social worker uses her announcement voice. "Well, Jewel, I am aware of the best services available for you, especially in your fragile state of mind."

Jewel gets off the bed, stands in front of the three girls, and glares at the social worker. "What if I wanting to go to this group with them? You not stopping me. I thinking for myself."

The social worker taps her cheek with a finger. "Well, I'm not sure. That would take a lot of extra paperwork on my part to make this alternative group happen."

"That's why you done college for. To learn the paperwork. Why you think you telling me how to, to, to . . ."

Teresa moves behind Jewel and whispers, "Recover."

"Yeah, recover from this . . ."

"Trauma," Marisela says.

Jewel looks to Marisela; she nods her head. "Yeah, this trauma, if I not knowing the people. But if I already knowing some of the people at this trauma . . ."

"Group," they all say.

"This group, better for making the talk easier."

The social worker stops tapping her finger on her cheek. "Well, I'm not sure. I would have to check if there is any space for you."

Teresa steps next to Jewel. "We already checked, and there is. That's why we came." She looks down and moves back a step.

Jewel crosses her arms and puts on a stance of rebellion, daring the social worker to go against them.

"Okay, if you're determined to do it your way and not take my advice . . ."

"I going where I deciding to go." Jewel thrusts her crossed arms down like a period.

"Okay, but for now, we have a doctor's appointment."

Marisela moves up. "May we go? It might be a little easier for Jewel if she has friends with her."

"Friends?" The social worker and Jewel say at the same time.

Wasted Ships
by Jewel

Friendship. Friends? Friends!
Fiends?
They look so pretty in all their niceness.
They're not fooling me. I'm not suckered by their sincerity.
They think I owe them now? They think they own me?
I'll hang with them now?
They'll show me how it is to be female?

Rule #47
Receiving love is sometimes the hardest to do

The hospital nurse points at a door with three numbers on it.

Jewel stands in front of it. The door stays shut. She reaches up and knocks quietly. Nothing happens. She turns to leave.

"Come in."

Darn, he's awake. She pushes the door open and peeks around the door.

He waves her in.

Jewel steps inside and almost gets hit when the door swings shut. She moves to the side and stays close to the wall. The officer has his right arm and shoulder buried under a cushion of bandages.

He looks at her but does nothing.

She stands and sticks her hands in her pockets.

He wiggles his finger for her to come over.

She watches her feet go across the ugly linoleum. She goes slow, and when she reaches his bed, he's still alive. She feels distress over his colorless face. The machines beside the bed click and beep and sputter like they're alive. She counts so many tubes, she can't tell where they all go. She touches one. It's cold. She follows the length of the tube with her finger, and the tube ends at his hand. She snatches her hand back. "Sorry."

Raúl Ortega says, "You have some explaining to do, young lady."

Jewel sighs. Some things never change. "I going now. Just checking if you still alive."

He grabs her hand and holds it weakly. "I want to talk with you."

Jewel zooms on his hand holding hers, and her heart wants to pump out of her chest. "I not done anything. I just getting here."

In a raspy voice, he asks, "Why did you put yourself in danger like that?"

Danger? She's in as much danger when she's at home. It's the same thing, just a different face. She wants to yank her hand away, but she's afraid she'll hurt him.

She stares at him. She feels her mouth open. "I coming to see how you doing, and you starting in on me." She curves her body away from him. "Are you for real? No wonder your son feels like he got to be fantastic to get you to notice."

Mr. Ortega says some words she's sure she doesn't want to know what they are.

She yanks her hand away. She doesn't care if it hurts his hand. "You know anything about being human? How people like you get to be parents, I not ever know."

He points with the hand that has the tube. "Listen, you did well, but don't get smart with me." He coughs. "I owe you." He coughs again. This time the coughing doesn't stop.

He folds up, holding his arms across his chest. More coughing. Like he's fighting for air. Sweat runs down his face.

She's scared. The coughing eases. Slows to hacking. Stops.

Mr. Ortega points to the pitcher of water. Jewel picks it up and holds the straw for him to sip. After she puts it back, he says, "You."

"No, you listen. Listen to what your son do. He does good at school, and you want more. He does good with his friends, and you question them. He makes plans, and you got no clue. Believe in what you know is good in him."

He glares, wetting his cracked lips.

"You got to listen to what he do. Got to believe in him. Julián got to have you believing the same for him like you believing God. With faith."

"I already do." The words sound like a snarl from a hurt dog.

"Not where he can see it." Jewel points to her heart. "Not where he can pack it up and take with him wherever he goes, to have handy for him."

He closes his eyes and breathes long and deep. He stays like that for a while; then his hand jumps to catch her hand and holds it. This time with gentleness.

"You make it sound easy."

"No. Not always easy. It not got to be so hard either. Just love him and believe in him. And tell him. Often."

Mr. Ortega rolls his head to cross-examine her. "Who loves you, Jewel?"

She smiles. "My mom always loves me."

"She believes in you, too?"

Her smile flies away. "She hurting. I believing for the both of us."

Mr. Ortega swallows and licks his lips. "It took a lot of guts for you to come today."

She shrugs.

He offers to shake her hand. "How if I got believing for you?"

They laugh so hard, the nurse comes in to scold them.

Wasted Parents
by Jewel

Parenting is the hardest job in the world.
Comes with no directions.
Most want to do it right.
Most think they are doing it right.
Most have the love.

With the stuff of earning daily bread,
paying bills, fitting the needs of
each person into their life—
partner, boss, friends, their parents, kids—
the love thins.

For some people it's impossible.
For others it's so easy.
Some people work too hard at it.
Some do what was done to them.

For some people they want to do different
than what they got and go way
overboard to the other side.

Love grows.
Multiplies the more you give.
Give it and receive it.

Sometimes receiving love is the hardest part of all.

Rule #48
Good-byes always hurt

Noises from the Elkins' kitchen float up the stairway and through the closed bedroom door.

"Jewel, I need you to sit down."

"Why?"

"I have something to tell you." From across the room, Jewel flinches at the words, and Grace jerks in surprise.

Grace remembers the day she was notified about her parents and how everything was dark then, too.

"I not liking the way you sound." Jewel moves slowly toward the window.

"You can stand if you want, but I have to sit down."

Grace moves to the bed and sits down. She worries over the expectant reaction from the child dressed in floral-patterned tights. Grace smoothes all the wrinkles from the white chenille bedspread. If she could only clear the wrinkles out of Jewel's life this simply.

Grace puts her hand to her stomach to ease the cramps and hears the child she was, crying and being told she had to be strong. Strong, in her family, was the one sign of goodness.

Jewel stands with her back to the window and examines the social worker. "That's fine. You not got to tell me nothing."

"Yes, I do."

"No, you not. I know already."

Grace springs to attention. "Who told you?"

"It about my mother."

"Who told you?"

"Her dead, right?"

Grace nods and notices how pale Jewel becomes against her dark hair. "You hadn't heard?"

"I always knows when it my mom. Something between us." Jewel turns around and stares out the window. "How her do it?"

"Overdose."

"On purpose?"

"Not sure." Grace stands up, reaches for Jewel but stops. "Is there anything I can do?"

"My mom happy. Her okay now. I know if her not."

Grace steps closer. "This had absolutely nothing to do with you."

"You know not a thing."

"No, it's true."

"Her trying to kill herself since I a baby. Her look to me to protect her safest."

"You're the child. It was *her* responsibility to look after you."

"Her so full of love and hope. At the same time, her got just as much pain." Jewel sobs. "I work hard. I accept the latest. I not ever figures out what I able to do for her to makes it any easier. I not able to save her."

"Honey, there is nothing you could have done. This was her choice."

"Not gives me crap." Jewel wipes her wet cheeks with the back of her hand.

Grace reaches into her purse.

"People like you look at my mother and think she got nothing. I nothing because I hers." Jewel blows her nose with the tissue that Grace hands her.

"You're hurting yourself."

Jewel faces out the window. "She's so scared of the world."

Grace pulls out another tissue from her purse and dabs at her eyes.

"She dead. I nothing."

Grace searches for the words to calm Jewel. "Your mother tried the best she could."

"I couldn't make her see."

"I understand you're angry. That's to be expected."

"I ain't angry; I disgusted. You so hot, you get to fix it all, Social Worker Lady?"

Jewel vibrates with anger so fierce that Grace steps behind her. Jewel wraps her arms around her stomach and grips her sides.

"You ever having someone hold you until the pain goes away? You telling that person they important to you?"

Jewel stares out the window. The branches from the nearby tree reflect on the window over her face.

Grace moves closer. "Jewel, I'm going to touch your arms."

Grace touches Jewel's arms, then wraps her arms around Jewel and hugs her. Jewel remains stiff until they rock together for a few minutes. Then Jewel lets go and leans back on Grace.

Holding the girl's weight, Grace's cheek is against Jewel's head. She speaks softly, "You're important, Jewel. You're very important."

At the funeral home, Jewel arrives with two bags. She hands one of the bags to the funeral director. He checks inside the bag and eyes the scarlet-sequined dress. "This is pretty fancy for a burial. You sure your mother would have wanted this dress?"

Jewel nods. "It's a favorite of hers. I remember her wearing it when I was little and she was going out."

The funeral director eyes the frail girl and wonders how much smaller she could be.

"The shoes too." She points in the bag he's holding open to a pair of silver high heels. "Don't forget to put on her watch also.

Those diamonds spell out her name. See?" She points to the chips along the band.

He nods.

She inspects the contents of the bag once more. "That's it."

He places the bag on his desk.

"Can I see which casket she'll be in?"

"Are you sure you can handle it?"

Jewel glares at him, and he steps back. "Right this way."

In the showroom, she stands in front of an oak casket. She reaches inside and touches the satin lining. "She likes the color ivory. It'll make her hair show up pretty." She presses on the bottom of the casket. "I want to make sure it's soft enough for her. It has to be very comfortable. She likes where she sleeps to be comfortable."

The man steps back, steadying himself for an outburst.

From the second bag, Jewel takes out the foot-long purple feather. She waves it across the length of the casket, back and forth, and recites, "Evil spirits away with you. Only angels and good fairies visit my mother forever." Then she places the feather inside of the coffin. "She'll need this. It'll protect her from dragons. Make sure it stays with her."

Jewel walks out the door, then down the sidewalk. The funeral director stands in the doorway and follows her with his gaze. He is unsure of what to make of the small person with the stiff shoulders, who brought her mother a book of directions on how to play Bridge.

Rule #49
Love conquers all in the head

Julián slides through the propped open door into his father's hospital room. His father is ashen. Julián moves to the end of the bed and stands.

He has been summoned by his father. Julián doesn't know what he's done wrong now. But he's afraid to wake the supine man. The doctor reported his patient would be as good as ever. But he finds the man he looked up to all his life lying in bed, tubes sticking out of his arm and hands. This makes Julián doubt the best specialists. His father has always been on the side of right, even if Julián hated what he heard. This man has always been invincible. Now his father, like any other man, could die.

"Come closer. I'm not in my coffin, yet."

Julián jumps. "Thought you were asleep."

"I was, but I could hear you thinking, and it woke me up."

Julián moves closer to the bed. "I thought you were going to die."

"Wasn't too sure myself."

Julián stares, his mouth hinges loosening. He transfers his gaze to the clipboard above the bed. It has his father's name on it.

"Better close your mouth. You're attracting flies."

Julián shuts his mouth with a click.

"Tell me what's going on in school."

Julián shifts his body into protective mode. "I haven't been in any trouble."

"You're a good boy." Raúl coughs. "Any trouble you get into, you can handle. I want to talk about your studies. What are you going to do when you graduate?"

Julián's surprise is quickly replaced with caution. "You're not well."

"Well enough."

Julián sways his weight from one foot to the other. "You won't like it."

"You're telling me what I think."

"You do it to me all the time." Julián snaps his mouth shut. The words escaped before he had a chance to edit them.

"You're right. I do."

This time, Julián takes a step back and eyes the man in the bed. "You have a fever?"

"Nope. Just trying to do things differently."

"Gunshot messed with your brain?"

Raúl laughs and grabs his bandaged shoulder.

Julián moves closer and touches his father's arm.

Raúl slides his hand over his son's and tightens his grip.

Julián returns the grip steadily.

"You have the strength of a man. I have to start thinking of you that way." Raúl holds their clasped hands up in the air. "You're getting to be your own man now." He lowers them and gently holds his son's hand. "I've had a hard time accepting that you were growing up. I was afraid of losing you."

"So by driving me away, you thought you'd keep me?"

"Not too smart, eh?"

Julián's eyes sting from staring so hard at his father.

"I want to make it clear that I believe you're a good man. Whatever it is you're doing in school, you'll do just fine at it."

"It's about college. I've applied, and they tell me it could be . . ." Julián hangs his head. "But I didn't apply to the police academy."

"Good thinking."

Julián double takes with his mouth in an O as big as his eyes.

"Do you think I want *this* to happen to you?" Raúl waves a hand at his shoulder. "I've worked this hard so you could do something better."

"But, all the time, you talk about how this city needs more Chicano cops. How this world isn't going to get better unless more Chicanos get involved."

"Doing what they love to do. Yes, it's important to get involved. Being a cop is only one way. My way. Maybe not your way."

Julián doesn't utter a sound. He can't.

"Whatever you decide to do, if you do it with good reasoning behind it, I'll back you up 100 percent."

"You haven't heard . . ."

"I know you. That's enough."

Julián opens his mouth.

"Wait. I have one more thing I want to say. I should have said this more often. But sometimes being a parent can become so much of a job, you forget it's the little . . ."

"Just spit it out, Dad," Julián urges, quietly.

Raúl smiles. "I . . ."

The door opens, and a nurse glides in rolling a loud clattering cart full of bottles and packages. "Visiting hours are over. Your son will have to leave, Officer Ortega. Time for your medication. Do you need help?"

"My son will help me." His words shoot out in snapping order.

"Visiting hours are over. It's regulation."

In a voice Julián is very familiar with, Raúl says, "My son will leave a few minutes after you do."

The nurse's gaze skims from the father's stern face to the son's smile. She bangs the noisy cart out the door. On her way out, she retorts, "I'll be back in fifteen minutes to give you your medication."

Julián and Raúl laugh. "Dad, don't worry. I'm taking care of Mom."

"Thank you."

"I better go." Julián pulls his hand away.

Raúl holds his hand tight. "I wanted to tell you . . . I just wanted to say . . ."

"The nurse is coming back, Dad."

"Son, I love you."

Julián gasps, taking a step back, then leans over and hugs his dad. "I love you too, Dad."

Raúl wraps his arm around the boy's shoulder and pats his back.

Julián straightens up, sniffing. "I have a lot to tell you. They have this research project I may be able to work at this summer. It will really help me get into college."

"We have plenty of time to talk." He points to his shoulder. "I'm going to be here for a while. Come over after school."

"Great. All right." Julián gives his dad another quick hug and heads for the door.

"Son."

Julián stops at the door and faces his dad.

"Bring Jewel with you, too."

Julián stares.

"She's all right. I want to make sure she has plans for after high school."

"Sure, Dad."

Julián steps out into the hallway and bumps into the nurse.

"Excuse me." Julián points with his thumb at the room he just exited. "Did my father suffer any brain damage?"

Wasted Touch
by Jewel

Do you remember the first time
you were touched as an infant?

When the fingers trembled
for fear of you breaking.

When you were a
precious bundle
bringing joy
and wonder.

When the most important
thing was to hold you
gently, tenderly, not
to rile you, just
to please you.

When did that stop
being important?

When did it stop to
matter if we were
being gentle
with others . . .

Or with ourselves?

Rule #50
Knowing about families
isn't the same as working at being a family

Grace opens the door to their apartment. The only light on is in the bedroom. She heads toward it and stops at the door. Glen has his suitcase open on the bed, clothes scattered around.

Glen looks up. "They've wanted me to take this training seminar in Utah for a while now. I've been avoiding it, but this time I decided to go. It'll give us some time to think about us."

"Leaving soon?"

"Soon as I can. I don't have a reason to stick around." He points to what she has in her hand. "Your briefcase is full. You'll be busy for the rest of the night. I'll get out of your way."

She steps into the bedroom. "Glen?"

He looks at her. Waits.

She opens her mouth. Being hit by a train couldn't hurt more than pushing these words out.

He goes back to his packing.

She steps up and touches his back.

He stiffens, then continues packing.

"I have a gift from Jewel. For you."

Glen looks puzzled. "What does she have to give me?" He throws a pair of sneakers into the suitcase. "Is she putting a hex on me because you're moving her to another school?" He searches through his drawers for his favorite socks.

"No. I've changed my mind about that."

When he turns back toward the bed, he catches his wife still staring at him. "Good."

He tosses the socks into the suitcase. He flips it shut and snaps the latches. He lifts his suitcase and walks to the foyer, where he sets the suitcase next to his briefcase and laptop bag.

Grace follows him, her hands clasped at her chest. She says the words in her head. She can mouth them in her mind. She can open her lips. But the sounds refuse to come.

"Glen."

He stops on his way to the kitchen and looks. He steps closer to her.

Can he puzzle out what she wants to say? Can he judge how much she wants him to stay? Can he appreciate how lonely she's been? She attempts to force the words out.

"Glen."

"Yup, that's my name. Don't wear it out." He searches her face.

She reaches out for him in her heart. Read me. Hear me. Know me.

He raises his arm and tenderly touches her arm. "I love you."

"Please rescue me." She covers her mouth with her hand. That wasn't what she wanted to say. "Don't leave."

Glen stoops to be eye-level with her. He lifts an eyebrow in question.

The smile she puts on is of low wattage. "I shouldn't say . . ." She licks her lips. "I'm trained to know better. No one can rescue me."

Glen smiles. "Give me a try."

She sobs.

He cradles her in his arms.

"Rescue me. Please rescue me." She leans her head against his chest. "That's so unprofessional of me to say." She looks up at him, then down at her hands on his chest. "You've been filling in the silences and . . . and I let you." Her shoulders shake with her crying. "Glen, I didn't know anyone wanted to hear what I had to say.

I locked my feelings away so long ago, I don't know if I can, if I will be able to, if I can give you what you need."

He pulls back and looks at her, his eyebrows doing the asking.

"I mean, what I need, too. I don't know how to ask for what I need. No one ever wanted to know before." She sniffles. "Funny. We've been married this long, and I never realized . . ."

He clears his throat.

"I never let myself realize how much I need to need."

"What brought this on? I mean, I hope it was the thought of losing me, but I think not." He gives his crooked grin.

"It was. I felt you slipping away, and I didn't know how to say don't go."

"You did fine just now."

She leans against him, exhausted from the depths of the emotions she's feeling. "Jewel. She said something."

He waited.

"She said I couldn't rescue myself by rescuing her." She looks into his face. "Has that been what I've been trying to do all this time? Rescuing myself. Did I do an injustice to all these children I've been working with?"

"Whoa there, Love. Don't take on the whole world again just as you're getting close to what is going on." He hugs her tightly. "All of us live our lives in some way or another. We hope we can find the part of us that we feel is missing. It's human nature. You," he leans back and kisses her on the nose, "have just done it in a way that has benefited a whole bunch of kids that no one else gave a damn about."

"Have I lost you?"

"Me? Oh, baby, it takes a lot to get rid of a Thomson."

"That's what your mother said. Long ago."

"Really? Well, mothers know best."

Rule #51
When romance works,
you're lucky, but when it doesn't...

Tom fumbles with the coffeemaker. His kitchen walls are decorated with paintings by Carol MacDonald, an artist he and Symonne met at MacDonald's annual Christmas sale.

"Is the coffee ready?" Symonne asks as she sets the table.

"Almost. Another minute."

Tom looks out his kitchen window and spots the two little girls playing with their dolls in their yard.

"What's so interesting out there?" She touches his arm with a finger.

Tom snaps his attention back into the kitchen and smiles at Symonne. "Nothing. Everything worth looking at is inside this room. Come here, I want to show you something."

He walks down the hall and into his office, looking back occasionally to reassure himself that she is following. "This is something Jewel wrote. I wanted you to read it. It's what made me send you the poems."

Symonne takes the paper, circles the room searching for a place to sit, and finding none, goes into the living room.

Tom trails after her and watches as she reads. He pinches himself. He never believed this woman would be in his home.

The sunlight tilts its way through the sliding glass door, and he feels as if he has been blessed with a new life. When she discovered he was the one who had written the poems, their conversation had charged off, ranging through different topics.

At first, he had been furious with Jewel, but as the prospect of rejection faded, he realized he owed her a great deal.

"I wrote the same thing. When I saw the words through her eyes, I knew I had to do something." Tom blushes.

Symonne leans over and kisses him on the cheek. "Jewel is a very special girl."

"So special. Why did she go to that apartment when she knew those scumbags hung out there? Didn't she know it would be dangerous?" Tom rubs the fabric on the back of the sofa.

Symonne pulls her concentration from the paper she holds, drops them on her lap, and reaches out for him. "Oh, Honey, it happens all the time. Girls that have been molested, as Jewel must have been, didn't get a chance to learn how to protect themselves and will inadvertently enter a situation that is obviously unsafe to most people, yet they don't recognize the danger at all."

"You know what? Maybe we can have some kind of celebration for Ronnie and his family and friends and make Jewel the guest of honor."

Symonne nods. "That would be nice. You could cook your fabulous eggplant dish."

They both smile as they remember how the eggplant casserole had grown cold at their first dinner.

"She deserves a reward for the great job she did with Ronnie. She worked hard, and he's doing great."

Symonne smiles. "Not to mention . . ."

Tom leans over and kisses her on the nose. "Not to mention the great job Jewel did in bringing us together."

"Why do you think she went to all that trouble?"

"Jewel is the last of the romantics. She has a heart so big, it just takes in the whole world. She is one special kid. I wish, heck,

I'm determined to find a way to get through to her. I'm going to make a difference in her life."

He pulls Symonne closer to him as she says, "We both will."

"I'll talk with Jewel tomorrow at school. What I have to say can wait until the morning."

Symonne smiles. "My theory is, when you have a good thought about another, tell the person right off. People need to hear that others think well of them. It adds value to their lives." She kisses Tom on the cheek. "Never hurts to say good job. Or well done. Or I really like you. Never hurts to let someone know you cherish them." She turns to face him. "Did you know that the opposite of abandon is cherish. It's never better to save your thoughts for tomorrow."

Tom embraces Symonne. "Seems like now is the time to tell someone they're wonderful."

Rule #52
All your answers are inside of you

"Did you catch my grade? I got it in the mail today."

"¡Híjole! That's the greatest."

Ronnie and Julián slap hands in the air. Julián jostles him across the room to the plaid sofa in the den of Ronnie's house.

Julián socks the cushion next to him as he extends his legs and sets his crossed ankles on the pockmarked coffee table. "You did it, *vato*. You did it. You're on your way to college."

Marisela runs down the stairs and sits beside Ronnie. She wraps her arms around his neck. "I knew you could do it. I always knew you could do it."

Ronnie's grin eats up most of his face. "It was a breeze."

Julián says, "Right. No trouble at all." Both boys laugh.

Marisela shakes her head at their foolishness.

Ronnie's cheeks outshine Rudolph's nose. "*Ay*, I got a gift for Jewel." He holds up a small, brightly wrapped package.

"What is it?" Julián asks.

"I bought her shoelaces for her high tops." Ronnie grins. "In fluorescent colors to match her hair."

Julián's gaze swings over to Marisela. "Is he for real?"

Marisela laughs. "I'm working on him, but you know how it is with these brainy types." She spreads her hands, palms up.

"You fool, Jewel helps you out of a bad spot, and shoelaces is all you can think to buy her."

"They're practical," Ronnie says.

"Flowers and other stuff are better, dummy," Julián offers.

Ronnie looks at Marisela. "Really?"

Marisela stiffens her neck. "Don't show up on my doorstep with any shoelaces. Fluorescent or not."

Ronnie looks back and forth between his friends. "It's all I bought."

Julián smiles. "Heck, you know Jewel will think they're great."

"I have to go tell Jewel about my score." Ronnie moves away from them.

"I'm going with you." Julián sits up. "I have a message from my dad for her. If you can believe that."

"What's he want to do? Put her in jail?"

"No, man, he wants to talk to her about signing up for the police academy."

"No way!"

"No lie, man."

"Did the bullet ricochet off your dad and hit you in the head?"

"Man, I wouldn't be able to make up anything this wild on my own."

"Ain't that the truth. Let's go tell Jewel. Now we have two things to celebrate. Without her, none of this would have happened."

Rule #53
Never underestimate your power of touch

Jewels are precious. Rare. Jewels require a lot of care. Most people aren't able to provide so much caring.

I pull out the stash of pills I've had hidden in my smelly sock. Every house I've been in had some kind of medication. I gaze at the different colored pills in my hand.

The phone rings downstairs. It won't be for me.

These pills in my hand take up more space than I do. I'm nothing in this world. I push out my hand and touch emptiness.

People cross paths all the time. They meet. They say, "How do you do?" Their lives are different for having met each other. I meet people, but I don't make a difference. I'm invisible to others. Just a pawn to move on a chessboard. I can't think how my living makes another's life better. Even a tiny bit.

I swallow all the pills. I'm a mistake. No one wants my mom's throwaway piece. Sleeping is the best medicine. By the time I fall asleep, the game will be over.

The ambulance pulls away from the house. The blue and red lights flash pale in the sunlight. The siren blares. Cars don't move out of the ambulance's way.

Ronnie wipes his eyes as he wraps an arm around Marisela's shoulder. Julián sniffs and looks in the opposite direction from where the ambulance is going.

Even though the sun shines on them, Mrs. Elkins rubs her cold arms. "I'll go call the social worker."

Norma leans against the porch railing. "Shit." She slaps the railing. "Shit."

Marisela looks up at Ronnie. "You never got to tell her." She hiccups with tears. "She never found out how much she helped you." Red blotches appear on her cheek.

Ronnie wraps his arms around her and holds her tight. "It's okay. She'll be okay. Really."

Julián pats Marisela's shoulder. "Ronnie's right." He sighs. "I don't think she ever knew how she touched other people's lives."

Rule #54
Rain and funerals make you run for cover

The weather is perfect for a funeral. The drizzle softens everything to a blurry day.

The six of them trek up the slope to where the service is being held. Ronnie and Marisela huddle under one umbrella, Julián another.

Their yellow rain slickers are the only bright color.

They reach the service. The priest nods to them and continues his prayer. An altar boy holds an umbrella over the priest's head.

The rain was unexpected, so the ground crew did not have a chance to set up a canopy. Mud runs down into the grave. Rain pelts the tarp that covers the pile of earth. Rain beads up on the oak casket, flows down the edges, and drips to the ground like teardrops. The single floral spray droops under the weight of collected raindrops.

They spot their homeroom teacher and the health teacher standing close together, and the three of them look at each other. They would grin if the circumstances weren't so solemn.

The social worker Marisela had met before stands on the other side of the casket. Next to her, with his arm around her shoulder, stands a tall, good-looking man.

Deano holds the umbrella for Norma and Mrs. Elkins, who is proper in all black.

The three of them look at each other, then across the casket. They feel bad. None of them knows what to say. The drizzle taps soft on the casket.

The priest closes his book. The altar boy swings the smoking censer toward the casket. Everybody looks at Jewel.

Drenched, her purple sweater sags to her knees. Her hair is plastered around her face. She stands. Alone.

On a signal from the priest, Jewel steps up and drops a rose on her mother's casket. The back of her hand is covered with tape over a cotton ball from the IV.

The priest speaks to Jewel, but she doesn't reply. She doesn't even look at him. He nods and walks away, followed by the altar boys.

The three of them, led by Ronnie, circle around the hole in the ground.

Ronnie says, "We wanted to be here for you, Jewel."

Jewel doesn't look at them. "What for? So you go back to school and tell everyone how the orphan's holding up? I not need you."

Marisela steps up and takes hold of Ronnie's arm. Julián tugs Ronnie's other arm to steer him away. They walk toward the car.

Tom Garner moves in front of Jewel and kneels on one knee. "You have to let someone in."

She doesn't look at him. "I got no one now." Seems like she doesn't even blink.

"It's a matter of trusting the love to be there for you. Just like you taught me." Symonne moves behind Tom as he says, "Jewel, I care. You touched my life and made a difference. Let others make a difference for you."

Jewel stares at the casket.

From the other side of her, Grace says, "You taught me something. Now you're going to make the same mistake I made. You're going to close yourself off because you think alone is safer? Your mother taught you better. Remember? As long as there is love, there is hope. God loves you. We love you. Those kids love you."

"We all want to be your friends. That's why we're here. Get it, Jewel. People like you. We want to be here for you. Let us," Tom adds.

"No." Jewel snaps. "My mother never loved me. She might want to look like she loved me, but she was always too busy with herself to care about me. She's gone now. I can admit it. I don't have to play her games anymore, hoping for scraps."

"You deserve much more than scraps. Let others into your life. Let someone care about you for a change."

All of them look toward the road where the three kids huddle around the family station wagon Julián drove.

Tom touches Jewel's shoulder. "Go on. Join the others."

Symonne puts her hand on Tom's shoulder. He gets up and puts his arm around her waist.

Jewel angles around the grown-ups and trudges toward the road. She walks slow, watching the three teenagers at the car.

First one, then another, then all of them turn to watch. She stops in front of them.

She doesn't move. She doesn't appear to breathe. The rain drips from her hair. The breath she needs to say the words hurts her chest. "Think I can catch a ride home with you?"

Ronnie looks at Marisela. She squeezes his arm. Ronnie says, "Jewel, you can sit on my lap, if you want." Ronnie opens the door and lets Marisela slide in. He stands at the door and looks at Jewel. Julián goes around to the driver's door. He gets in the car and starts the engine.

Ronnie sits down and sticks out a hand. "C'mon, Jewel."

Jewel steps stiffly toward the car as if the rain has frozen her body. She gets into the car and sits between Ronnie and Marisela.

Marisela hands her some Kleenexes.

Ronnie takes the tissues and wipes her face. "You know, crying at your mother's funeral is considered very macho."

She cranks her head and faces him.

Ronnie grins. "Especially when you're with friends."

Jewel scans his face like she's studying for an exam.

Ronnie puts one hand on her back and, with a gentle pressure, draws her toward him.

She leans against his body and puts her head on his shoulder. Stiff.

She shivers from the cold, so hard her body shakes. Ronnie puts his arms around her and holds her tight. Marisela holds Jewel's hands.

The shivering slows.

Ronnie hums as he pats her back. Tears mix with the raindrops on Jewel's face.

"We're friends, Jewel. Friends," Marisela says.

For the first time, Jewel understands what the word "friends" means. She hangs on tight to Marisela's hands.

About
The Chicano/Latino Literary Prize

THE CHICANO/LATINO LITERARY PRIZE was first awarded by the Department of Spanish and Portuguese at the University of California, Irvine during the 1974-1975 academic year. In the quarter-century that has followed, this annual competition has clearly demonstrated the wealth and vibrancy of Hispanic creative writing to be found in the United States. Among the prize winners have been—to name a few among many—such accomplished authors as Lucha Corpi, Graciela Limón, Cherríe L. Moraga, Carlos Morton, Gary Soto, and Helena María Viramontes. Specific literary forms are singled out for attention each year on a rotating basis, including the novel, the short-story collection, drama, and poetry; and first-, second-, and third-place prizes are awarded. For more information on the Chicano/Latino Literary Prize, please contact:

Contest Coordinator
Chicano/Latino Literary Contest
Department of Spanish and Portugese
University of California, Irvine
Irvine, California 92697